SKINNY PUNK GENIUS SAVES FAT KID

"Lucky for you I was at that station," Curt says as he watches me eat. "I mean, since I saved your life and all." His eyes track each bite I take, but when I offer him my fries he won't take any.

"I wasn't going to jump," I say, holding a french fry in the air. I'm lying, but only halfway.

Curt scoffs.

"Were," he says as if there's no argument. "I was watching you for, like, an hour. That rude, twirpy kid left, then three trains passed and you never looked up from the tracks. Then the insane laughter and I knew you'd lost it. I said to myself, Curt, you save this kid's life and he will surely buy you lunch."

"I wasn't going to jump," I say again with my best resolute look. I was just thinking. Just *thinking*."

Curt considers this at length.

"How come?" he finally asks.

I want to give him the you-moron look the kids at school have perfected. Maybe say something sarcastic like, "Use your imagination." I want to say, "Open your eyes. I'm a fucking three-hundred-pound teenager living in the most unforgiving city on earth. I'm ugly and dumb and I make stupid noises when I breathe. I annoy and bewilder my only living parent, mortify my little brother, and have no friends."

I shrug.

OTHER BOOKS YOU MAY ENJOY

aimee	Mary Beth Miller
Bronx Masquerade	Nikki Grimes
Catalyst	Laurie Halse Anderson
Miracle's Boys	Jacqueline Woodson
The Outsiders	S. E. Hinton
Postcards from No Man's Land	Aidan Chambers
Stetson	S. L. Rottman

fat kid rules the world

K. L. GOING

speak

An Imprint of Penguin Group (USA) Inc.

PUFFIN BOOKS
Published by the Penguin Group
Penguin Young Readers Group, 345 Hudson Street, New York, New York 10014, U.S.A.
Penguin Group (Canada), 10 Alcorn Avenue, Toronto, Ontario, Canada M4V 3B2
(a division of Pearson Penguin Canada Inc.)
Penguin Books Ltd, 80 Strand, London WC2R 0RL, England
Penguin Ireland, 25 St Stephen's Green, Dublin 2, Ireland
(a division of Penguin Books Ltd)
Penguin Group (Australia), 250 Camberwell Road, Camberwell, Victoria 3124,
Australia (a division of Pearson Australia Group Pty Ltd)
Penguin Books India Pvt Ltd, 11 Community Centre, Panchsheel Park,
New Delhi - 110 017, India
Penguin Group (NZ), Cnr Airborne and Rosedale Roads, Albany, Auckland,
New Zealand (a division of Pearson New Zealand Ltd)
Penguin Books (South Africa) (Pty) Ltd, 24 Sturdee Avenue, Rosebank,
Johannesburg 2196, South Africa

Registered Offices: Penguin Books Ltd, 80 Strand, London WC2R 0RL, England

Published in the United States of America by G. P. Putnam's Sons,
a division of Penguin Putnam Books for Young Readers, 2003
Published by Speak, an imprint of Penguin Group (USA) Inc., 2004

10 9 8 7 6 5 4

THE LIBRARY OF CONGRESS HAS CATALOGED THE G. P. PUTNAM'S SONS EDITION AS FOLLOWS:
Going, K. L. Fat kid rules the world / K. L. Going
p.   cm. Summary: Seventeen-year-old Troy, depressed, suicidal, and weighing
nearly 300 pounds, gets a new perspective on life when a homeless teenager
who is a genius on guitar wants Troy to be the drummer in his rock band.
[1. Obesity—Fiction. 2. Musicians—Fiction. 3. Interpersonal relations—Fiction.
4. Drug abuse—Fiction. 5. Suicide—Fiction. 6. New York (N.Y.)—Fiction.]
I. Title. PZ7.G559118 Fat 2003   [Fic]—dc21   2002067956
ISBN 0-399-23990-1

Speak ISBN 0-14-240208-7

Designed by Gina DiMassi. Text set in Charter.

Printed in the United States of America

1.

I'M A SWEATING FAT KID standing on the edge of the subway platform staring at the tracks. I'm seventeen years old, weigh 296 pounds, and I'm six-foot-one. I have a crew cut, *yes a crew cut,* sallow skin, and the kind of mouth that puckers when I breathe. I'm wearing a shirt that reads MIAMI BEACH—SPRING BREAK 1997, and huge, bland tan pants—the only kind of pants I own. Eight pairs, all tan.

It's Sunday afternoon and I'm standing just over the yellow line trying to decide whether people would laugh if I jumped. *Would it be funny if the Fat Kid got splattered by a subway train? Is that funny?* I'm not being facetious; I really want to know. Like it or not, apparently there's something funny about fat people. Something unpredictable. Like when I put on my jacket and everyone in the hallway stifles laughter. Or when I stand up after sitting in the cafeteria and Jennifer Maraday, Brooke Rodriguez, and Amy Glover all bust a gut. I don't get angry. I just think, *What was funny about that? Did my butt jiggle? Did I make the bench creak so that it sounded like a fart? Did I leave an indentation?* There's got to be something, right? *Right?*

So it's not a stretch to be standing on the wrong side of the yellow line giving serious thought to whether people would laugh if I threw myself in front of the F train. And that's the one thing that can't happen. People can't laugh. Even *I* deserve a decent suicide.

That's why I'm standing here. Because I can't make up my mind. I'm thinking about what Dayle said. *Go ahead . . . I wouldn't miss you. Go ahead . . . Go ahead . . .* I'm telling myself my brother didn't mean it, but even I know that's a lie. Meanwhile it's hot and I've been standing too long. . . . I close my eyes and imagine the whole scene as it might play out.

First, the train is coming, its single headlight illuminates the dark tracks. I hear its deep rumble and take the fateful step forward.

I want to picture myself flying dramatically through the air but realize I wouldn't have the muscle power to launch my body. Instead, I would plummet straight down. Maybe I wouldn't even get my other leg off the platform—my weight would pull me down like an anchor. That's how I see it. The train plows into me; my fat busts apart, expands to cover the train window and the tunnel walls. I'm splattered. Except for my left leg, which is lying on the platform untouched—a fat, bleeding hunk of raw meat.

FAT KID MESSES UP—coming soon to a theater near you.

I start to laugh. Suddenly there's something funny about it. I swear to God. There really is.

2.

"YOU LAUGHING AT ME?" The disembodied voice is clearly addressing me.

"Huh . . . ?!" I turn away from the tracks.

"You're laughing at me?"

"No . . ."

Who the hell is talking to me? I have to scan the entire subway platform before I find the voice. Twisted staircase, black gum-covered tile walls, infested concrete pit . . . and then, ah, the source of the paranoid voice. He's right beside me, but he's sitting on the floor, which is why I didn't see him.

He looks like a blond ferret. Stringy unwashed hair and huge eyes, jeans that are barely recognizable, stained white T-shirt, huge red overshirt, ratty old sweater . . . The sneakers, one Converse and one Nike, are both untied and the layers are all partially buttoned even though it's got to be one hundred degrees in the subway. The guy is so filthy I can hardly look at him. I mean, he's caked—looks like an old war victim from some black-and-white film.

There's one more thing I notice—and if I'm telling the truth I should admit that I noticed it first. He's the skinniest person I've ever seen. Even in all those layers, the kid is skinny.

"You mocking me?" I say, angry. I want to say it with a snarl, but when your cheeks are puffy you don't snarl, you huff. A little puff of air escapes despite my best intentions and I end up sounding like an overweight dog farting. My eyes dart and I think, *Did that sound funny?*

The kid laughs. His face wrinkles and he looks even more like a ferret. He says, "Now *that* was funny." Except he doesn't hold his nonexistent stomach and howl, and he doesn't try to keep a straight face to be nice while obviously choking on suppressed hysteria. He says it straight-out. Makes me think. A little puff of air while I was trying to be tough? I guess it is funny. The dirty, skinny kid got it right.

I'm ready to give him full credit and be on my way, mosey along to contemplate some new nonfunny form of suicide (FAT KID GETS HIT BY A BUS?), but the blond ferret stands up and extends a grimy hand.

"Curt MacCrae," he says. That's when I just about piss my pants.

Curt MacCrae is a legend at W. T. Watson High School. He's the only truly homeless, sometimes student, sometimes dropout, punk rock, artist god among us. He's the only one who's ever played a concert at The Dump. The only one that bands like the Trees and King-Pin *invite* to hang with them. He's the only one to get into five fights in one day, get the crap beaten out of him in all five, and still have everyone's respect. He's the only fucking genius guitar player I've ever met. And, of course, he's the only one to get up in the middle of class on a Tuesday and disappear for good. Kids at school loved that.

Since then, no one's actually *seen* Curt MacCrae, and that was last year. The school newspaper took a poll and three-quarters of the student body think he's dead. Everyone refers to him as the Blair Witch of the Lower East Side. And I just shook his hand.

"Troy," I say. "Troy Billings." It comes out starstruck and I frown a little to compensate. "I know your music. I mean, I heard a bootleg of a show you played with Smack Metal Puppets. It was so great. Really great. Really, really great."

Curt makes a face, then glances at the tracks. He walks sideways two steps and cocks his head, thinking hard. The F train speeds into the station and the Sunday afternoon crowd climbs into the empty train. I should've thrown myself in front of it, but now I'm left standing there, awkward.

"That's my train," I say. I need to split before I do anything stupid. Anything *else* stupid.

Curt grins. "Hell it is."

"What?"

"You owe me lunch."

"What?" This, the only word in my vocabulary.

He hops twice.

"I just saved your life. It's the least you could do."

He says it matter-of-factly and I'm confused. I'm standing there sweating and I wonder if I smell. God knows he does. He reeks.

"I owe you lunch?" I say, further solidifying the impression that I am a moron incapable of conversation.

"Yeah. *Mmm-hmm.* Handicapped elevator's this way." He shrugs in no particular direction and takes off. I'm insulted about the elevator comment and he's completely wrong about saving my life, but I'm hungry and by some freak occurrence in the universe Curt Mac-Crae appears to want to have lunch with me. So, I go.

3.

WE EMERGE OUT OF DARKNESS into bright sunlight and Curt points like an explorer declaring land in the distance.

"Diner," he says, as if the word explains it all.

I'm way out of breath, so I just nod. I think about catching a cab back home, maybe just handing Curt the money for lunch. I haven't eaten in a restaurant since ninth grade, when Dad dragged Dayle and me to his military retirement dinner. It was a fancy restaurant and I had to wear a suit. A fat kid in a suit is definitely funny. But this is worse. Huge Fat Kid and filthy, skinny, blond ferret. Half of New York City stops to watch. Curt is oblivious, intensely focused on the diner's front door.

"How much money you got?" he asks as we wait to be seated. I'm thinking this isn't such a hot idea even if it is Curt MacCrae. I'm thinking I should have jumped.

"Twenty," I say. I really have thirty.

The waitress approaches and gives us the look—the one where her eyebrows shoot up to half the height of her forehead. At this point she makes an effort to control them by turning them down into motherly concern. Doesn't work. She doesn't look like a mom—she's got big hair, big earrings, and big breasts.

"You boys want a seat?" she asks, as if it's something special she's doing just for us. Curt doesn't hear. He's too busy rubbing his hands together like one of those madmen in the old monster movies. Dr. Frankenstein bending over a collection of body parts.

"Twenty, huh?" He licks his lips and grins, slides into the booth beside the window even though the waitress is clearly leading us to a table in the back. He picks up the menu and stares at it like a wild man. Somehow his staring does not give the impression that he's actually reading. He stares too intently at one spot.

I force my body in across from him and catch several men at the counter watching us. They look away and I think this place feels cramped and smells like alcohol at 2:00 in the afternoon. I think, *I'm about to eat lunch with Curt MacCrae at a Bleecker Street dive.* Me and the psycho Elvis of rock, hanging out. *Not bad for the Fat Kid, right?*

The waitress comes back with our waters. She's wearing one of those authentic-looking diner outfits. Short black skirt, white blouse. The buttons on her sleeves are undone and when she sets down our glasses I can see her bare wrists. *Erotic.* I'm practically salivating just looking at them, but Curt says "Grilled cheese" before she's even set his glass on the paper place mat. She smiles and the eyebrows go up again. Curt takes a deep breath.

"And french fries," he says, then contorts his face as if he's just made an agonizing mistake. "No," he says with resolve. Then, "Yes." "No" again, then, "Damn, damn, damn, shit. Yes. French fries and ketchup. Lots of ketchup. Oh, man." Curt grins so big I think his face will split and the waitress laughs. I make a mental note. *Skinny blond kid excited about food. Very funny.*

"And for you?"

The waitress wants my order. Is she mocking me? God, I want to touch her. Her legs are full and long and if I could just reach under that skirt . . . I need to control myself. *Must. Not. Be. Sex. Starved. Loser.* A drop of sweat lands on my menu. I stare at it, then wipe it off with my shirtsleeve.

"Same, no fries," I say. I try smiling to compensate for my uncontrollably lewd thoughts, but my cheeks turn red and I huff instead. The waitress doesn't seem to notice. She's too busy smirking at my order.

"Are you sure?" she asks.

I'm not. In truth, I want to order everything on the menu but can't stand the pressure. I'm convinced everyone is secretly watching me and no matter what I order I cannot win. Too much and they'll nod knowingly. Too little and they'll think, *A bit late for that, now isn't it?* I huff again before I can help it and with the release of that little puff of air I think, *Aw, screw it.*

"Give me the french fries," I say, "with lots of ketchup."

Apparently that's the correct answer, because she nods and heads for the kitchen. Once she's gone I want to make small talk, but Curt's too distracted. I ask him a bunch of questions about music, things I've always wanted to know, but all I get is "Hmm" and "Yeah" in no particular relation to anything I ask. Furthermore, every time we nearly make eye contact Curt's head whirls around as if someone could be getting away with the Great Food Heist behind us. Watching him makes me motion sick, so I give up all attempts at conversation until the food arrives.

The waitress sets down the plates of grilled cheese and fries and Curt actually gets tears in his eyes. He leans close to the table and puts his dirty head near the food. It appears as if he's listening to it. The waitress hesitates. She can't keep her eyes off him. For that matter, no one in the whole goddamn diner can take their eyes off him.

Curt goes straight for the ketchup bottle. He pours a dollop of ketchup onto his spoon and eats it directly.

Watching Curt eat is somewhere between appalling and torturous. It's appalling because he puts so much ketchup on everything. I imagine I'm eating lunch with Hannibal Lecter. It's torturous because he enjoys it so much. He's extremely emotional about everything he eats.

"Well . . . uh . . . you boys . . . yell . . . if you need anything."

Our waitress backs away for fear she will miss something. I can't blame her. I don't touch my food the whole time Curt is eating. No one but the cook makes any noise while Curt fills his skinny body with ketchup and processed cheese. The world stops while the skinny kid eats. *Fuck that,* I think. But I also think, *God I wish I were him.* . . .

When he's done Curt leans back, drums on the table with one finger, and practically weeps again. The waitress has been hovering and now she asks if he wants dessert. Curt looks up as if he's surprised to see us, then shakes his head.

"No, thank you," he says. The waitress leans forward.

"Are you sure?" she asks. "On the house?"

"Can't," he says, then looks at me. "Besides, Troy hasn't eaten yet."

He's right. For once, I haven't eaten a thing.

4.

"LUCKY FOR YOU I was at that station," Curt says as he watches me eat. "I mean, since I saved your life and all." His eyes track each bite I take, but when I offer him my fries he won't take any.

"I wasn't going to jump," I say, holding a french fry in the air. I'm lying, but only halfway.

Curt scoffs.

"Were," he says as if there's no argument. "I was watching you for, like, an hour. That rude, twirpy kid left, then three trains passed and you never looked up from the tracks. Then the insane laughter and I knew you'd lost it. I said to myself, Curt, you save this kid's life and he will surely buy you lunch."

He says all this with a deadly serious expression and I wonder if he's mocking me. But it makes sense. Why else would someone save the Fat Kid before he takes the leap? And Curt does appear to be starving.

"I wasn't going to jump," I say again with my best resolute look. "I was just thinking. Just *thinking*."

Curt considers this at length.

"How come?" he finally asks.

The question is absurd. Unless he means how come I decided against it. But I don't think he does.

I want to give him the you-moron look the kids at school have perfected. Maybe say something sarcastic like, "Use your imagination." I want to say, "Open your eyes. I'm a fucking three-hundred-pound teenager living in the most unforgiving city on earth. I'm ugly and dumb and I make stupid noises when I breathe. I annoy and bewilder my only living parent, mortify my little brother, and have no friends."

I shrug.

To which Curt shrugs back. We sit together in silence, then he stands up quick.

"Oh, man, I'm sick," he says. "Shouldn't have had the french fries." He slides out of the booth and disappears, leaving me stranded, wondering how my life became so absurd.

5.

I'M CONVINCED HE'S SHOOTING UP in the bathroom. Maybe he is. Who knows? All I care about is that it's tight in the booth and I'm sweating again. Any minute now the waitress is going to come over and see me perspiring like I've just run the New York City Marathon. I imagine her face as she hands me the bill. A grimace. Maybe she doesn't even hand it to me, just drops it on the table.

I wish I were home in front of the television. It occurs to me that my brother is home already, thinking I've killed myself. I wonder if he'll be disappointed.

There's time to pay the bill and slip away while Curt's in the bathroom. I agonize over the decision and by the time I look up to signal our waitress I see Curt instead. He slumps across the diner and slides back into the booth, curling into one corner.

"Order something else," he says. "I don't feel good. We gotta stay until I feel better."

We? I think. But he really doesn't look good. Still . . .

"I've got to get home, Curt. I'll order you something else, but my father is expecting me."

Curt looks directly at me for the first time since the subway station. "Come on, man," he says. "Please? I gotta stay until I feel better. Just order a soda or something."

It's the "please" that gets me. No one has said please to me in a long time. There's something about being fat that makes everyone think they're doing *you* the favor.

I look to our waitress, who is barely restraining herself from coming over now that Curt is curled into a tiny ball, stick-thin arms twisted around filthy jeans. He's confined to one-eighth of the bench. The exact width of one-half of my butt cheek.

I nod. "Okay."

Curt grins and reaches deep into one pocket. He pulls out a pile of lint and a whole slew of tablets. Of course they're not drugs. Drugs don't come in individually wrapped pharmacy-sealed silver packets, do they? Maybe they do. I freak. I've never seen drugs before and I can see the headline: FAT KID ARRESTED FOR POSSESSION. Beyond humiliating.

Curt sees the look and scoffs. He holds up one foil packet and says "Imodium" really loud. "Not heroin. Imodium." Then he grins, having cracked himself up. I blush with embarrassment. I'm not going to ask him about the other pills, the ones that are *not* Imodium. Not after that. Besides, Curt's too pleased with himself and I'm too mortified.

Curt closes his eyes and chews the tablets, then leans his head back and settles in.

After a while he says, "Let's just state from the beginning that I don't have AIDS or some mysterious disease. I'm not dying. I'm not even homeless all the time. No one beats me or fucks me without my permission. Got that?" He pauses. "This isn't some after-school special where you learn to love yourself by saving my sorry ass. I saved you, remember? Let's keep that straight."

My eyes can't find a single safe place to look. I'm so red I've turned purple and I keep making that stupid huffing sound. Curt digs farther into his pocket and rescues a cigarette butt from the lint. He relights it and takes what would be a long drag if the butt weren't so bedraggled.

"I like to lay things on the line," he says. "Life ain't Hollywood." He curls up tighter. "Life is shit."

6.

I WANT TO LEAVE, but Curt wants to talk. He's entered this strange zone between hyper and comatose. He runs his fingers obsessively through his greasy hair, but keeps his eyes shut the whole time he talks.

"Where do you live?" he asks. I shift nervously.

"Lower East Side. Just off Stanton Street."

"Yeah?" he says. "What school?"

"W. T. Watson."

"No shit?" One eye opens. "That was my school."

"Mmm," I say, unsure how to respond.

"Like it?" he asks.

The question throws me, in part because no one ever asks me that, but mostly because it seems legit, as if Curt's mind can honestly conceive that I, a six-foot-one-inch, three-hundred-pound seventeen-year-old could possibly enjoy public school in a city full of aspiring models. It's an astounding mental leap that cements in my mind the fact that Curt MacCrae really is insane.

"No," I say.

Curt doesn't respond. After a while he says, "I liked school. It was okay."

I'm thinking, *Of course you did. You had a band. You were cool. Everything you did was a statement. People wanted to be you.*

I don't say that. Instead I say, "Where do you live now?"

It seems like a fair question, but Curt hesitates, then starts obsessively eating all the saltines from the cracker basket.

"That's a good question," he says at last, tugging at a plastic packet. "And I can tell you the answer because I wouldn't keep anything from my friend who just bought me lunch."

It hadn't occurred to me that I'd asked a question one might not want to answer.

"Well, I didn't mean—"

Curt holds up a hand. "No, it's really very simple." He takes a deep breath. Shifts position.

"You see, technically, and this is only in the technical sense, legal court orders and all, so, yes, technically I live with my father, but that's hard to do, really, so I don't. You know, mostly 'cause he's kicked me out a couple times. And left. But that doesn't mean it's out of the realm of possibility that I could be living with my father. . . ." He pauses, thinks things over, reassesses. "And there are some aunts and uncles sometimes, too, but it's safe to say without *exaggerating* that they don't like me in the sense of the word 'like' that would imply you might be allowed to live with someone."

Definitely confused. I try asking a clarifying question. "What about your mom?" I ask, to which Curt nods vigorously.

"Well, yeah, of course that's where I live. Mostly." Another pause. "Except she married this asshole who"—he coughs—"is a *wife beater hypocrite asshole,* so really it's more like I *used* to live with her, but now not really some of the time."

I find myself staring at his lips as if I'm deaf.

"So, where exactly does that mean you live?" I finally ask. Curt shrugs, as if it's obvious.

"You know, all over. With my mom. In lobbies. Friends. Smack Metal Puppets."

The last is the name of a local punk band in the Village. I have everything they've ever produced, from demos to handmade posters, hidden in my sock drawer. It's hidden so Dayle can't make fun of me for liking them. They are amazing musicians—ultrahip in an emaciated, alienated sort of way—but if Dayle thought I listened to them he'd be on my case. So, I'm a closeted fan.

"Smack Metal Puppets?" I say, hopefully.

Curt sits up. "Yeah. You like them? Ever gone to a show?"

I can't help but stare, slack-jawed, before swallowing hard.

"No. I mean, yes. I like them, but I've never gone to a show."

Curt is animated for a second, then leans back and closes his eyes.

"Man. Big T, you should go. Raw stuff."

It's at this precise moment that I decide to stay as long as Curt wants me to. He doesn't know it, but he's just uttered the one word, the one letter, that will buy him whatever he wants for the rest of the day. Fat Kid just got a nickname.

Curt keeps talking, but the conversation is over. All I do is grin, hoping he'll say it just one more time.

7.

IT'S BEEN AN HOUR and Curt still hasn't said we can go. I've ordered two pieces of pie and eaten them both. FAT KID EATS TWO PIECES OF PIE. *Is this okay?* I wouldn't have ordered them except Curt asked me to. He said I had to buy him some time. Made me feel like we were in a spy movie, waiting for something big to happen. Except nothing big happens. Curt goes to the men's room and I'm left staring at two empty pie plates.

Curt gets up a third time, but I'm too embarrassed to order more pie. I settle for inconspicuously cleaning the plate, but the waitress slides in across from me just as I'm running my finger over the white plastic, scooping up the last of the cherry filling. I'm caught, red-handed, but it's too late to abort the mission.

"Who's your friend, sweetheart? Is he all right?"

God, she's hot. I sit there with cherry pie filling on my right index finger, trying to decide if I should lick it off or pretend it's not there. I compromise by wiping it on my napkin, hoping she won't notice, then wonder if someone as disgusting as I am will ever—*ever*—see a woman naked.

I clear my throat. "Yeah. He's all right," I say at last. "He just . . . gets sick a lot. He's got stomach problems and he doesn't get to eat, so when he does eat he gets too excited and it makes him sick."

"Does he need to see a doctor?" she asks. I can tell she wants to offer him money. Maybe clean him up and take him there herself. She doesn't know what to make of me, but she's sympathetic because I'm with him.

"Naw," I say, sounding like an expert. "He's done that before. He just needs to eat better."

She nods in agreement as the bathroom door at the end of the diner opens. She winks at me and slides out of the booth. I can feel the heat rising through my body as she leans in close.

"Tell him he can eat here anytime," she whispers, her hot breath on my neck. She walks away and I can't take my eyes off her. That's more attention than I've received from a female in my entire adolescence. I want to stay for the rest of the day, but Curt comes back and announces he's ready to leave. He's more subdued than he was on the way in, doesn't run around me in a circle as I pay the bill, but once we're outside in the glaring sunshine he sort of half jogs, half skips beside me. I'm mortified. SKINNY KID SKIPS BESIDE HUGE FAT KID.

Then I have to laugh. It comes out as a huff, then a chortle choked between my fat lips. Then I'm laughing so hard I don't give a damn. Curt's laughing, too, and I think for a minute, he understands.

8.

SO, NOW I'M STANDING ON the curb at Bleecker and Broadway trying to hail a cab. Five empty ones have passed and it's starting to annoy me. I've never enjoyed hailing cabs—something about raising my huge fleshy arm like a target, then stepping toward traffic—and most of them don't stop for me anyway. *Why stop for the Fat Kid when there's a skinny person one block over?* Usually I make

Dad do it, or take the subway, but at this point the thought of walking even one extra block is too much. I expect Curt to take the hint and leave, but he doesn't.

"So, uh . . . I gotta go," I say at last.

A yellow cab is finally maneuvering through traffic, cutting off a half dozen other cars in order to reach me. I can already see the driver—a Chinese guy—debating his decision. *What does he see? Huge freak with cab fare?* Curt pretends he doesn't hear me.

"What's your instrument?" he asks as if we have all the time in the world. I suppose in Curt's universe everyone naturally plays an instrument. I glance at the cabdriver and he glares, so I answer quickly.

"Drums. Junior high."

Curt nods appreciatively. "That is most excellent because the very thing . . ." His voice is lost in the drone of traffic as I shuffle forward. I have to walk around the cab because Curt is leaning against the door on the passenger side. Typical New York, everyone pretends they can't see me waddling into traffic. As soon as I attempt to open the door there's an explosion of car horns culminating in a bagel truck slamming on its brakes and the driver giving me the finger. I look over at Curt to see if he's noticed, but he's oblivious. His eyes are squeezed shut, his face is contorted, and he's playing air drums. Based on my miniscule confession, he's now demonstrating his all-time favorite drum solo.

"A *bam, bam, braaat, braaat, bam, bam, bam, braaat, braaat, bam, bam, braaat, braaat, bam* . . . and then this sweet bass line jumps in and it's *weeeehhh* . . ." Curt makes a high-pitched scream right there in the street and everyone who's been staring at us looks away. Desperate, I fling open the cab door and slide in quick as I can, hoping Curt's scream will mask my departure. Then I realize he's climbing in the other side.

"What are you doing?" I ask, but Curt pretends he doesn't hear.

I know he heard me because he raises the volume on his music mono-logue. I have to lean forward and shout to be heard by the driver as I yell my address.

Curt talks the whole ride home. He talks about chord progres-sions, then guitars. He names all the makes and models, then rates them. Then he lists them again in order of his rating. Then he changes the list and recites the *revised version* twice as if cementing it. He does the same thing, for my benefit I presume, with drum sets. Then he starts on bands.

It's only a few blocks, but by the time the cab pulls up to my apartment building I think I might strangle him. Not only is he driv-ing me insane but his stench is making me nauseated. I've tried to roll down the window without being too obvious, but when the cab stops, I bolt. I waddle over to pay the driver and Curt stands on the curb with his hands dug deep in his pockets. I hope he won't notice as I take out my hidden ten-dollar bill, the one I told him I didn't have, but he just stares at the pavement as the cabdriver grabs the money and steps hard on the gas.

I move onto the sidewalk and Curt and I stand there watching our cab disappear into the sea of cars making their way up and down Houston. The moment already makes the Awkward Hall of Fame, but as per my life, it has to get worse. Just when I'm thinking I've made a huge mistake letting this skinny kid follow me home, I see my little brother rounding the corner. Dayle's holding a basketball, drip-ping sweat, and it's obvious he's been shooting hoops at Roosevelt Park while he waited to find out if I'd killed myself.

He swaggers forward, with attitude, moving the way you're sup-posed to move when you live on the Lower East Side—the way I can never move. I think, *He fits here.* Unlike me, Dayle belongs in Man-hattan. He's good-looking, athletic, and he can fit in anywhere. Take Dayle to the Upper West Side and he'd be dating a stockbroker's daughter. Take him to the Village and he'd be playing football with the college kids at NYU. Me? I can live in the same neighborhood my whole life and still stand out like a sore thumb.

I watch him approach, wishing just once he'd trip and fall flat on his face. I'm dreading the moment he realizes Curt's with me, and sure enough the first words out of his mouth make me cringe.

"You have *got* to be kidding."

Dayle takes one look at Curt and knows I've done the wrong thing. Two roads diverged in a yellow wood and Dayle wishes I'd taken the one that ended in front of the train. He won't even look at me. He's not only disappointed, he's angry. He glares at Curt as if he's already intuited Curt's role in thwarting my attempt.

"Who is *this* loser?" he asks.

Curt breathes out slow.

"Ah," he says, like a guru on a mountaintop, "the rude, twirpy one."

Dayle sneers and I give him my "big brother look." The look hasn't worked for years—not since Dayle turned seven and started beating me in sports—but I always try it anyway. *Got to make the attempt, right?* That's what I think, but then I decide I'm kidding myself. *If I were Dayle, would I listen to me?*

He redirects the sneer from Curt to me.

"Now what have you done?" he mutters under his breath, managing to sound pissed and offended all at once. Ever since Mom died Dayle's been convinced I'm plotting to irreversibly humiliate him.

I clear my throat.

"Well . . ."

That's when my father comes out of our apartment building. We don't live in a big building, it's a shabby five-story walk-up, but Dad still stops to lock the security door just in case someone decides to break in while his back is turned. He strides over and plants himself in front of me.

There are now only two options as I see them. Curt can leave or Curt can leave. Elvis or no Elvis, the time has come. I wait for Curt to make his exit, but he doesn't move. My father gives him a single disdainful glance before focusing on me. Priorities. As usual, he radiates quiet disappointment. He's a neon sign advertising the Blue Light Special: *Disappointed Dysfunctional Parent. Disappointed Dysfunctional Parent.* I'm sure Curt can see it flashing. *Couldn't anyone?*

"Where have you been?" he demands. The question is barked at top volume, and from the corner of my eye I see Curt nod in appreciation. My Dad is an ex-Marine and he has terrific lung capacity. Dayle smirks and opens his mouth to say something rude, but Curt interrupts.

"Band practice," he says before anyone can answer. We turn as one and Curt nods, encouraged by our undivided attention. "Yup," he says, "band practice." I gape and he amends his statement.

"I mean, really just band formation, mental thought, planning today, but soon-to-be band practice of the most intense kind."

No one can translate what's just been said. I glance at Dad and his face is screwed up like a raisin. My dad is big, like me, but all muscle. Six foot, five inches of tall, lean Marine. Since he retired he does freelance security for rich people uptown who want their own personal commando. Dad fits the part. Like me, he keeps a crew cut, but his cheeks aren't fat and he never huffs. He is not, under any circumstances, funny.

"We're called Rage, or Tectonic, or Rage/Tectonic," Curt continues. "Sort of a punk rock, Clash sort of thing." He's making it up as he goes along, but liking what he comes up with. The hint of a smile plays at his lips. My father turns to me.

"Troy? Who is this?"

For a moment, the entire absurd day flashes through my brain and I know the only truthful answer is "I don't know." Then I think of every other pathetic day I've spent for the past seventeen years, and decide, just once, I'd like to pretend I'm in a rock band.

"Dad," I say, "this is Curt MacCrae."

A burst of laughter explodes across the street, and one of our neighbors yells something in Spanish. I swear they're laughing at me. I picture the scene as everyone else must see it. Huge whale of an unsplattered Fat Kid, emaciated piece of dirty blond twine, repressed bewildered military machine, and Dayle. Three freaks and a normal kid standing on the sidewalk.

My brother looks like he wants to sink into the concrete. I almost feel sorry for him, and I wish he might find the whole thing funny. I mean, it is funny, *isn't it?* But I can tell he doesn't think so.

I shift position and my thighs rub together. No one says a word, and in the absence of a response, my mouth gets diarrhea.

"Curt's played with a bunch of bands, and they're all really good. Nothing you guys would've heard of, of course, but that's only because you don't listen to that kind of music, but it's all hidden in my sock drawer, or it *was,* but now I'm going to take it out, so you might hear it sometime. Curt's amazing on guitar. . . ."

Curt grins. "And vocals," he adds. "I do awesome vocals."

I nod. "And vocals."

My father's eyes narrow.

"Shit," says Dayle.

Dad glares at him while I rush to say just *one more thing.*

"I didn't tell you about Curt before because I didn't want you to get mad." This is pure B.S. and Dayle knows it.

"He's lying," he whines, but Curt shakes his head.

"Not," he says. He glares at my little brother as if he might squash him. Dayle's got muscles like Dad, but he's little and I almost think Curt could win by stench alone. Finally, Dad sighs.

"Dayle," he warns. Then, like a good soldier, he regains the tension in his jawline and focuses on me. "If you were meeting your . . . friend," he says, "you should have told me." He turns to Curt, his attention directed at him for the first time. I hold my breath wondering what he'll say. Will he think Curt's too good for me? Tell him to find someone else to play drums in his band?

My father's eyes narrow.

"You," he states, "are unacceptably dirty."

Dad glances toward our apartment and Dayle's eyes bug out.

"Dad, you've got to be kidding. We can't let *him* use our bathroom. I swear, only Troy could pick up such a loser. If anyone at school hears about this . . ."

He stifles the last thought before he utters it, but there's an awkward moment while my father and I look at the ground. Curt just smiles directly at Dayle. It's funny to watch my little brother get so pissed while Curt looks so smug. Makes me pervertedly happy. It's The Battle of the Skinny Kids now playing on the Fat Kid Channel. I want Curt to win even though he's skinnier.

Dad ignores Dayle and heads toward the apartment. Dayle and I automatically fall in line behind him, even waiting in rough formation while he unlocks the security door, but Curt follows in a meandering path, nearly getting locked out, then taking the steps two at a time once we're inside. He pokes his head around the corner on each floor, stops and starts about ten times, darts down the hall to inspect our neighbor's welcome mat, then has to jog to catch up. I think, *Damn, it's only two flights of stairs and a hallway.* Dad doesn't say anything, but I know it bugs him.

Once we're inside he makes Curt sit in *one place* while he gets him a bathrobe, towel, and new set of clothes. The clothes will never fit, but that doesn't stop Dad from declaring that everything Curt is wearing must be disposed of. Curt's face turns horrible shades of white and I think he might pass out, but he doesn't say a word. Only coughs twice.

Despite this, Curt looks supremely happy as he walks down the hall from the living room to the bathroom. He stares at every picture, and there're a lot of them. The apartment is filled with pictures of our family and in every one of them Mom's beautiful. She's always smiling and her long, dark hair makes her look Mexican. She looks nothing like my father, brother, and me. I watch Curt studying her and wonder what he sees. *Does he think I'm adopted?*

When Curt finally disappears into the bathroom, Dayle explodes.

"You can't really think you and this homeless kid can start a band. Where did you meet him anyway? He smells. He's a freak. He's worse than you, Troy. Almost worse than you. No one's really worse than you because you're such a major loser."

I swallow hard. My little brother doesn't get the fact that this is Curt MacCrae. He's not just *any* homeless person. He's a school legend. If Dayle weren't a freshman jock he'd know that.

"You're too young to remember," I say, "but Curt was real popular at school a couple years ago. And he's not homeless all the time."

My cheeks huff while I talk. Dayle pouts.

"Troy, you're the king of morons. You haven't played drums since seventh grade, and you weren't even good then. You don't own a drum set. You can't be active for more than five minutes before you're out of breath. Who do you think you and this Curt person are going to play for, anyway? You never go out. I swear to God . . ."

I could drop the lie right there, but I don't.

"Curt's a great musician," I say instead. "You'll see, Dayle. He's going to teach me everything he knows and Rage/Tectonic is going to be huge. Just wait."

Just wait.

9.

I NEED SERIOUS MENTAL HELP. What kind of person lies about being in a band when it's obvious that this is absurd? I mean, *what the hell was I thinking?* What did I imagine would happen?

I try conjuring the possible results of my lying.

First possible scenario: Curt comes clean. Literally and figuratively. He comes out of the shower racked with guilt and confesses on the spot. He tells Dad about saving my life. Dad tells me it's time to go back to the psychologist. Not the young one with the fabulous tits who made the hour seem like an X-rated movie. No, the old one who breathed like he had emphysema and couldn't think of anything more creative to ask than "Do you miss your mummy much?"

Scrap that.

Second possible scenario: I come clean. A week has passed and Curt is lounging around the house in my father's robe eating the maraschino cherries Dad keeps stashed behind the entertainment center. Dayle starts harping on me about my negative drumming talent and I crack under pressure. I confess to being a serious punk rock wannabe and everyone, including my father, laughs at my ability to delude myself. He kicks Curt out and Curt tells everyone connected to the music scene that I am—literally—the biggest loser he's ever met. They write a punk rock song about me and it contains the chorus *Split a gut, split a gut, laugh until you split a gut. . . .*

I'm ill.

Out of desperation, I conjure a third and final scenario that involves neither of us coming clean. This time, I pretend to be Curt's drummer until some future date when Curt loses interest in me. That would be tomorrow. Tuesday at the latest. Curt hangs out and eats free food, then he splits. No one's surprised, but no can say it's *my fault.* No one could say I didn't try, right?

The choice is clear. FAT KID MAKES AN EFFORT.

10.

FAT KID PROVERB #12: A clear choice is still worth agonizing over.

I pace the halls outside the bathroom door. Curt takes forever to shower, but when he opens the door, there I am waiting for him. A truly pathetic display of neediness. A blast of steam hits me in the face and Curt emerges like a rock star from a dry-ice fog. If he weren't the only other person in our house I wouldn't recognize him. He's entirely whiter, blonder, and skinnier than anyone could have imagined. Curt MacCrae has raised the bar on my dreams of emaciation.

Holy shit, I think, *he's concave.*

Curt ignores me. He walks to the living room while simultaneously trying to pull a T-shirt over his head. The T-shirt is one of Dad's and it reads MARINES in block letters. It's way too big and Curt can't find the armholes. He crashes into the wall, straightens himself out, then settles on the couch next to Dayle. Immediately, he picks up the remote control and changes the channel from ESPN to Comedy Central.

Normally, Dayle throws a fit if someone changes the channel, but today he's too busy staring to notice. Not only is the T-shirt too big, but Curt's also trying to wear a pair of Dad's pants that are approximately eighteen sizes too large. He has them rolled at the waist to keep them from falling down. Even so, the pant legs drape past his feet onto the floor. He's an elf transported to a land of giants.

Dad comes out of the kitchen, glances at Curt, and scowls as if it's entirely Curt's fault the clothes don't fit.

"Unacceptable," Dad says at last. He motions Curt toward the kitchen. "Just . . . just . . . just sit over there and eat something. Troy, get your friend something to eat. I'm going out."

Dad sticks his wallet in his back pocket. By all appearances he intends for Curt to sit and eat until he grows to a more acceptable size.

As opposed to an unacceptable size, of course.

11.

HMM . . . WHAT TO DO. When Dad says to do something, I do it. Ever the obedient Fat Kid, I start looking for food I can force-feed Curt. Only Curt has no intention of staying put. As soon as Dad's out the door Curt makes a low whistle and goes straight to the garbage can. He fishes out all his clothes and throws them into the kitchen sink. I watch, one hand suspended over the loaf of Wonder Bread, as he turns both faucets on full blast.

There's something about the days-old food rinsing off the shredded, splattered denim into the silver sink that's enormously pleasing. I almost point it out, but Curt's looking annoyed and Dayle's lingering in the doorway, so I keep my mouth shut. Curt turns to me. He appears to be concentrating very hard.

"Here's what we're going to do," he says as if picking up on a conversation we just recently left off. He speaks only to me, as if Dayle's not even there. "We're going to get you to a show or two, possibly four, then we're going to find you some drums, one of the well-rated sets to which I referred in the cab. *Eh-hem.* Now, I imagine your dad'll spring for a set if he's convinced that we're serious, which, of course, we truly are. And being serious, as we are, we'll make plans to pick up my guitar from my mom's place and start jamming when she and the asshole are at work. When I think you've got it, it being the technical drumming part of course, we'll pick up some gigs. . . . We'll plug ourselves by word of mouth now, you know, to build an advance buzz, see? That way, by the time we get our first gig everyone will think we're well-known and we will have successfully . . . *emm,* yes."

Curt ticks off this mental list as if the items are mathematical principles easily organized into an equation. Dayle rolls his eyes.

"If I *lived* here," Curt continues, "it would be way much easier for us to practice. *Very* beneficial. But, I don't know, I mean, I don't think your dad would go for that. But in a while, when he likes me, well, then . . ."

Dayle makes a choked gasping sound and his eyes bug out like a kid about to bite it in a horror movie, but Curt doesn't appear to be the slightest bit tempted to acknowledge him. He continues talking while I watch in awe.

"So, I'll meet you at, shall we say, school, in the morning. I'll talk us up, you'll skip for practice, and it'll be a sweet deal."

Just like that. All wrapped up.

"You two have got to be kidding," Dayle growls. He's shifting his weight from one muscle-toned leg to the other. My gorgeous, perfect, in-control little brother might just piss his pants. I grin. It's the Fat Kid's moment in the sun.

Curt smiles slyly, then continues ignoring him.

"Worst class?" he asks.

Is he serious? I glance at Dayle, but the question seems legit.

"Gym," I say. Curt thinks hard.

"*Mmm-hmm*. Gym. When's gym?"

"Third period." More thinking.

"*Mmm-hmm*. Third period. Before and after?"

I narrow my eyes. Answer carefully. "Math and study hall."

Curt nods like a Mafia kingpin closing a deal. He articulates his next question very slowly, so I know it's important.

"Are you . . . *good* . . . at math?" he asks. I wait an equally long time before responding, giving the question my full attention.

"Yes," I say decisively. I should leave it at that, but when you're fat you cannot miss an opportunity to prove yourself. "I'm good at all my classes except gym," I add. Then I curse myself because it's not true. I failed metal shop.

Curt nods, unaware.

"Excellent," he says. "You'll skip math, gym, and study hall every Monday. . . ." There's the briefest of pauses before he asks his next question. I expect it to have something to do with the plan, but I'm wrong.

"You got any . . . cough medicine?"

The question is so totally unrelated I think I've heard him incorrectly. I don't respond and he coughs, almost as an afterthought. I shake my head. Curt shrugs and the mood pops like a cherry.

12.

THE NEXT MORNING I WAKE UP with a start and look around for Curt, but there's no sign of him. I think I remember meeting him yesterday, but now I'm not so sure. I've woken up from reality convinced it was a dream.

My breath tastes like the bottom of someone's shoe after he's stepped in dog shit. If I have to be fat couldn't I at least have minty-fresh breath? I get up and pull on clean underwear and tan pants. I would shower, but I barely fit inside and I hate flooding the floor. Pisses Dayle off. And Dad. I settle for lots of deodorant.

I pick up a T-shirt that's wadded behind my stereo and smooth it against my leg. When I lift it to my face and sniff I realize it's the same one I had on yesterday. Smells like Curt—body odor and subway grime.

I put it on because it's my only tangible evidence that Curt MacCrae really exists. Like a man who's met God, I now question my memory of events. Did he *really* say his name was Curt MacCrae? Maybe that's just what I wanted to hear. Was he *really* at my house? Perhaps my brain, boggled by the stress of a thwarted suicide attempt, released powerful chemicals to convince me of a delusion. Did we *really* eat at a diner and pretend to form a band?

I lumber to breakfast, Fat Kid on a mission.

We sit down to eat and I annoy even myself with my incessant questions and my need to confirm reality with the only eyewitnesses I can find.

"Last night, when Curt was here, did you think the television was sort of messed up?"

"When Curt was in the kitchen didn't you think he looked a lot different?"

"Did Curt say something to you about the clothes you bought him?"

Dad and Dayle are less than helpful. Dayle no longer looks curious, he looks repulsed, and my father, well . . .

"Troy, pass the salt," he says, exasperated. He's too embarrassed to look at me.

"Yeah, right, Dad. Sorry." I snort. *Could I be more pathetic?* I take a tenth pancake. A second helping of eggs. Bright yellow egg yolks swirl with deep red ketchup on my plate. I decide to chalk up Curt MacCrae's presence in my life to a sick joke.

FAT KID HALLUCINATES ABOUT COOL FRIEND. Not funny, just sad.

13.

DAD DRIVES ME TO SCHOOL and, as always, I'm a surreal spectacle. He double-parks so I can get out, and the kids on the street stop to laugh.

What's so funny? I think. *Is it so funny every time you see it? Me getting out of the car? Dad waiting? What?*

I try to ignore them and think about what I'll do this afternoon when I get home. I decide which TV show I'll watch, then think about next Sunday, when I will think up some new way of committing suicide. Something less public and more inevitable. FAT KID DIVES OFF THE FIRE ESCAPE?

I concentrate on willing everybody away from Dad's car until he's driven off. Then I concentrate on getting inside the building with the minimum amount of sweat and breathlessness. Trust me, it's an ordeal.

In fact, it's such an ordeal that as I walk down the hall toward my locker I think about nothing else. Just one leg, other leg, first leg, second leg, don't huff, don't sweat, don't trip. Breathe.

Then I see Curt—a mirage in the distance. He's leaning against my locker surrounded by a small group of senior Goth kids. They're gathered around him in the same manner people gather around a gruesome car accident, gaping unabashedly, black figures profiled against red lockers, staring in a daze at what they could become.

I stare, too. I stop in the middle of the hallway and stare like he's an apparition that will fade if I glance away. Jocks and cheerleaders have to go out of their way to get around me. Classroom doors open and shut. The loudspeaker crackles ominously.

I think, *Curt MacCrae is standing at my locker. The real Curt Mac-Crae, not the least bit dead, is holding court at my locker.* Then I whisper, "There is a crowd gathered around my locker." The corners of my fat mouth twitch.

I take a careful step forward. The Goth kids are talking, mostly to each other. I hear the words "marijuana" and "band," but nothing evokes a response from Curt. He just stands there, studying his sneakers, chipping paint from my locker, kicking at a wad of gum on the floor. Every now and then he glances up and nods shyly.

I ache, *ache, I tell you,* to know how he does it. How does one person transcend everything about himself with so little effort? How does he pull us in like a magnet? He's as skinny as I am fat, but people love him. They want to surround themselves with him.

And of course, there's not enough to go around.

For a moment, I hate him. Then he sees me. Curt grins a lopsided grin and I move forward, caught in his tractor beam.

The crowd notices me and for the first time I feel the weight of their eyes. I whisper to myself, "Do *not* screw up. Do *not* trip. Do *not* huff." It's my big debut. There are girls watching and every single one of them is hot. I glance at them out of the corners of my eyes, start to sweat, and have to force my gaze forward.

Curt is motioning me to hurry up. He hops and paces, and as soon as I'm within arm's length he pulls me aside even though people are still talking to him. He drags me to the end of the hall and we stand next to the emergency exit door. A rampant grin runs away from my puckered lips as I wait for Curt's secret information.

"Practice, second period?" he asks.

I wait, confused. *After all that hopping and hurrying that's all he has to say?*

Curt takes out a couple pills and swallows them dry. Tilts his head back, and runs his fingers through his hair.

"Tylenol," he says when I don't ask. "Headache."

I wait for more. Something about the band. Something important. I wait for a prediction of my future, the meaning of life, the secret handshake of initiated music lovers everywhere. When nothing comes I think, *Tylenol?*

Suddenly it seems clear that this is not really happening. I may be deluded, but that wasn't Tylenol and I can't play the drums. It occurs to me that I'm the world's biggest moron and this is the world's biggest practical joke. Maybe everyone's waiting for him to deliver the punch line.

Did you really think I wanted to form a band with you?!

But Curt doesn't deliver his line and no one laughs.

In fact, this is probably the first time since fourth grade that I'm the center of attention and no one is laughing. An ironic development. I even see Dayle lingering with the rest of the freshmen and staring in my direction *without laughing.*

I hesitate. This might be my last chance to avoid, yet again, becoming the laughingstock of the entire school. I should walk away before it's too late, throw myself out the window before Curt has a chance to turn on me. It's the only choice that shows a hint of self-respect. I pause.

A hundred eyes stare in our direction and Curt shuffles in place, waiting for my response.

I open my mouth. . . .

If you think I walk away, you need serious help. *No, no, no, Cherie.* I say nothing rational, logical, or ethical. I make no grand pronouncements about personal integrity. What do I do? I turn *ever so slightly* so that my back is toward the hall and answer very carefully, dragging out my response for full effect.

"Second period," I say, nodding gravely. I make a hand motion worthy of the Godfather, and the deal is struck.

14.

CURT TOLD ME TO WAIT by the hoops, so I'm waiting by the hoops. Only he's not showing up. Second period is almost over and there's no sign of him.

Suffice it to say, I no longer feel like the Godfather. I'm a lonely fat kid waiting beside a graffiti-gouged wall and a barbed-wire fence—the Norman Rockwell painting for the twenty-first century. The way it looks now, humiliation is right around the corner, and I'm starting to get nauseated. I'm just about to go back inside when Curt finally arrives. He's in a rush and for a moment I think someone is chasing him. I watch, flustered, as he bangs into the fence.

"Come on," he says, rubbing his nose. "Let's go. Let's go. We've got to catch the subway. Let's go, man." He hops on one foot like a cartoon character whose legs keep moving when they're about to go really fast. Then he takes off again, weaving through cars, pedestrians, and an entire construction crew. By the time he notices I'm not behind him he's halfway across Second Avenue. He stops in the middle of the road and nearly gets creamed by the crosstown bus.

Curt stands there, scanning for me, while people honk, swerve, and yell obscenities out their windows. When I finally reach him he grins and says, "That was a close one. Didn't realize you weren't behind me."

I follow him to the subway and we ride downtown to East Broadway. As soon as we get off again, Curt leads the way, winding through a half dozen side streets with no street signs. He barely manages to walk slow and I barely manage to keep up. It's a miracle we make it there, and as soon as we arrive I realize it will be a miracle if we make it out again.

My neighborhood isn't exactly the posh area most people envision when they think of Manhattan, but Curt's street takes grime to a whole new level. It features metal security grates, stray cats in heat, loitering men, and empty vodka bottles, and there're at least three bars within sight at all times. There's not a single tree that isn't strangled by plastic bags or fried chicken bones. It's distorted and grotesque and I nod approvingly. *Maybe this is where I fit. . . .*

Curt blends in, skulking along as if he's guilty of some crime. When we reach his mom's place—the profanity-covered wall to the left of the Chinese restaurant—he looks over each shoulder, then picks the outside locks in a single swift motion. He has to pick three locks in order to get in, two to get inside the building and one to the first-floor apartment once we've stepped inside the foyer. I've never witnessed a crime before and this strikes me as a key moment in my adolescence. I stand two feet behind him the whole time trying to act nonchalant. Nonchalant three-hundred-pound Fat Kid—not easy to pull off.

Then Curt's on his way in, shoving open the peeling green door marked APT. #1 and kicking aside a stack of dusty books that fall when the door opens. There's a red neon AN IQUES sign in the window and it bathes the apartment in an eerie glow. Curt flicks on the light and the room is revealed to be overflowing with miscellaneous, ornately tacky objects. It's so full we can barely fit inside. There's a busted piano on one side of the room and no less than three velvet couches on the other.

"This is where you live?" I ask, but Curt doesn't answer.

"You live here?" I say again. There's something about the place that doesn't seem right. It's claustrophobic and chaotic at the same time. Reminds me of the junk shops in the Village where every inch of space is occupied with objects bearing no relation to each other. Here a golden elephant, there a crystal-framed mirror. The only sign that this place has some connection to Curt is the guitar lying under the piano. Curt nods at it, as if he's saying hello, or taking inventory, but he doesn't take it out. Instead, he leads me around three glass cases, two of the overstuffed couches, and several giant carved antelope.

"Home sweet home," he says at last.

15.

THE PLACE ISN'T BIG ENOUGH for two people. Not when I'm one of them.

We pass through a tiny bedroom, a crowded living room, a narrow kitchen that smells like mold, and a bathroom that's smaller than I am. I get the distinct impression that the bathroom is Curt's main reason for giving me the tour, because he ducks inside and removes a bunch of plastic bottles from the medicine cabinet. He sticks one in his shirt and opens the other.

He flashes it. "See," he says, "legit."

I'm almost positive the name on the bottle reads "Hazel," so I hesitate, studying the pink plastic rosary beads draped around the toilet.

"What's it for?" I ask cautiously. I'm trying to be devious, which always fails.

Curt shuts the bathroom door and heads down a narrow hallway. I follow and a line of chipped paint flakes off the wall as I pass.

"Seriously," I say again, yelling behind him. "What's it for?"

Curt stops short and I almost plow into him. I have to grab the wall to steady myself.

"Listen," he says, fixing me with a stern look. "Don't get uptight." He pulls out one of the bottles he put in his shirt. "It's prescription. See? Prescription."

He hands me the bottle and it does, in fact, have his name on it. I try to force a smile, but my chin quivers with the effort. *Right,* I think, *prescription. I knew that. Didn't I know that?*

Fuck. I'm screwing everything up.

"Sorry," I say, turning into a huge inflatable dork. "Sorry."

For the briefest of moments Curt looks pissed and I watch my future spiral into the abyss. Then the emotion washes away as if it were never there.

"Never mind," he says, casually. "Besides, you have more . . . err . . . important, shall we say, *consequential* things to worry about."

I'm blank. "I do?"

Curt raises both eyebrows.

"Well, you've got a gig in five weeks."

It takes a long time for his words to register, then I stare dumbly. All thoughts of prescription medication disappear from my brain with the exception of an instant desire for Prozac. I can't help wondering if I heard him correctly because it seems entirely too cruel and arbitrary that Curt could have set something up between last night and this morning. Does the universe—even *my* universe—operate that way?

The answer is yes. *Of course* Curt set up a gig. *Of course* I am caught in my stupid, impossible, humiliating lie. And the clincher is that now, instead of lying in a vague sort of way using words like "band" and "drummer," I will have to lie in a very specific way, as in "I'll be playing a gig on Saturday, November thirteenth, at ten P.M."

My brain turns to mush and I develop a stutter.

"Wh-what are you talking about? Th-that's not true, is it? You're kidding, right?"

The words come out in a splurt, and Curt laughs in a high-pitched, breezy sort of way.

"Funny," he muses as his face squinches up. "Relax, T. No up-tightness necessary. I have plentiful . . . *eh-hem* . . . connections at The Dump, so I went over there after I left your house and, well, see, I pulled us some strings. But no worries . . . five weeks is *plenty* of time for a, shall we say, 'smart' person such as yourself to learn the drums, especially given your . . . *cough, cough* . . . background in percussion."

It's a masterful move. He's taken every subtle nuance of my lie at face value. Didn't I imply that I was smart? That I'd studied the drums? Didn't I pretend I was going to be in the band, which would naturally mean playing a gig?

I have no one to blame but myself.

The sweat drips down my tree trunk of a neck as I pray to the hot pink rosary beads for mercy on my soul.

16.

I MUST BREAK THE NEWS to Curt. *I am not a drummer. I am the Fat Kid. Nothing more. I have never been a drummer and will never be a drummer.* I take a deep breath.

I let it out again.

Shouldn't Curt know this already? Even Curt can't believe we will form a *real* band and play an *actual* gig in front of *actual* people. He must know he's making a monumentally huge mistake. After all,

I'm not a little thing that can be overlooked. I *am* the elephant in the room.

On the other hand, this is Curt. I may not know a lot about Curt, but so far he seems to have an unlimited capacity for denial.

Big breath in.

Curt, we need to talk. . . . I rehearse the speech in my head. *I was just playing along, I can't really play the drums, I get hives when people stare at me.* . . . I open my mouth but Curt interrupts. He's digging through a box of CDs, oblivious to my angst.

"What groups do you like, T?"

I silently curse at the use of the nickname. *Damn him.* The question seems totally unprompted, as if he's just thinking out loud, wondering what I like. No harm in that, right?

I pause. "Well . . . I . . ." Now I'm flustered.

Curt looks up. "Don't you know what you like?" His face is contorted with disbelief and he looks like a ferret again. "You said you liked Smack Metal Puppets, right?"

I blush furiously. I do, but there's something embarrassing about admitting it. Fat kids ought to be into groups that are kind of funny, right? Weezer? They Might Be Giants?

Curt studies me, then stands up and squeezes out of the room.

"Come on," he says, his voice drifting away from me. "You've got to . . . I mean, *right now* there is something you must listen to."

He leads me into the bedroom and there, buried beneath the rubble, is an old record player. It's covered in dust, but Curt wipes it gently with one dirty sleeve, leaving both sleeve and player dirtier than before. He turns and starts digging through a box of records.

"You will most definitely like me, I mean this—this thing about me that I'm going to tell you. Because, see, T, I can tell you don't believe we can have the most awesome band ever, fucking ever, with just the *slightest* bit of practice on our part. But that's because you are afraid to embrace your true punk persona, well . . ."

Curt pulls out the record he's been looking for and studies it solemnly.

"Check this out," he says. He holds it the way Dayle holds Dad's old football trophies—the ones we're not allowed to touch. He slides the record out of the sleeve and offers it gently, holding it up for me to look at.

"This," he says, "is what I grew up listening to." I peer forward, looking for the answer to what I'm not embracing that will allow Curt and me to form the best fucking band ever. I don't see it.

Curt takes the record away before I get a good look and sets it in place. He blows the dust off the needle and there's a scratchy sound as the music comes out of the speakers, grainy and weak.

I clear a spot on the floor next to Curt and sit my huge butt down very carefully. I'm expecting Iggy Pop or the Dead Boys, but what comes out is entirely more melodic. It takes me a couple minutes to figure out that we're listening to the Beatles. Curt grins in a lopsided way. He glances at his sneaker and his face turns pink like chewed-up bubble gum.

"When I was a kid, see . . . well, my mom used to play these old Beatles records all the time. Yeah . . . and my dad, my *father* I mean, taught me to play guitar, because he was a real kick-ass guitar player. But my mom, see . . . she taught me to love music. So I was three and Dad would be all giving me this shit, like, practice, practice, practice, but she'd come home and put on these records after work and she'd dance around the kitchen with a bottle of beer. . . ."

Curt stares at the record turning round and round on the record player and for a second I almost see somebody else, somebody who doesn't fidget and cough. Then he lifts the needle abruptly.

"Anyway, my point is, and this is the point I'm trying to make, is to like what you like, right? Because we've all got our reasons for liking and if you don't like what you like then you really aren't liking. So, if you like Smack Metal Puppets that's cool. But if you like Barry Manilow or Air Supply, then, hell, the power's still yours so long as you own it. Got me, T?"

It's an odd little speech, but the strange thing is, I do get it. Somehow if Curt MacCrae can grow up listening to the Beatles, then the Fat Kid can like the Screaming Banshees. I've just had my first lesson in Punk 101.

17.

CURT SETS THE BEATLES RECORD carefully back in its case and starts digging through the other boxes. Every now and then he pulls out something vintage. The Ramones. The Stooges.

He pulls off his sneakers and his feet reek. His socks are stained with everything imaginable and I try not to play "name the stains." Curt sprawls over the junk as if it isn't there and I can tell he expects me to do the same. I want to tell him I'm a blimp in a china shop, but after a while I forget to worry about it. Curt pulls out an original Sex Pistols album.

"Oh, yes," he breathes. "I used to listen to this when I was with my dad. . . ."

I can tell he wants to finish telling me the story, but he puts on the record and gets distracted. He leaps over me, an Olympic hurdler, then runs into the living room, grabs his guitar, runs back, plugs it in, and rips into the guitar part. He picks up at exactly the right spot without missing a note. The music screams and he imitates each of the Pistols, simultaneously playing everyone, including Johnny Rotten. Then he laughs because he knows he's insane.

Meanwhile, I am a giant lump watching this virtuoso one-man performance. I don't even have it in me to be the audience. All I can do is ache until my skin feels parched and stretched from wishing I were him. He's on his knees leaning backward, making crazy punk rock faces and I swear he doesn't give a shit what he looks like. I know without a doubt that Curt would play this guitar part in the same way no matter where we were. Live and in concert.

I want that. *I want it bad.* I shift my huge rolls of fat until I'm poised to move.

But then it's too late. The song ends and Curt takes a couple ragged breaths before falling backward to the floor. He runs his hand over his guitar appreciatively.

"Shit," he says, "that was awesome."

It occurs to me then that the last time I let myself go—truly let loose—was a long time ago. In fact, it was third grade. Kelsey Drexler's birthday party right before my mom died.

Kelsey Drexler was the love of my preteen life, a cute little brunette, who'd invited me *personally*. Her little brother Wally started a water balloon fight and Kelsey and I ran around her yard half-naked, screaming bloody murder. I was eight and didn't know enough not to be insanely happy. Mom was still alive. I was still a twig. People liked me. It's been a lifetime and 230 pounds since I felt that way. Until today.

Watching Curt, I make a conscious choice to try to let loose. I don't throw myself around the room playing air guitar, but I do sing along and even scream a couple times when I forget not to. Curt cranks the music and every time a song ends we engage in vicious battles over what to put on next. I grin the whole time because no one ever fights with me anymore. Even Dayle just despises me loudly, but Curt swears up a storm when he doesn't get his way, which ends up being never because once he gets around to calling me a "fuckface bastard with no musical intuition" I always give in. I have the distinct impression he's enjoying my company.

All the while it's getting darker and darker, and in the back of my mind I'm worrying, truly I am, but I keep thinking, *Carpe Fucking Diem. I am the Fat Kid and I am having fun.*

18.

WHOEVER MADE UP THAT STUPID "seize the day" expression was never a teenager. Never a distorted mockery of a human being. There is no seizing. There is no control. Life gives, life takes away.

Everything changes when Curt looks at the clock.

"Shit, shit, shit, shit. We've got to get out of here." The clock hits the sixth chime and Curt morphs into Cinderella—the anorexic princess, not the heavy metal band with the big hair. He starts shoving records into boxes like a madman. He stands up, sits down, stands up again, gathers a bunch of CDs, lets half of them spill, doesn't seem to notice. . . . He's a flurry of motion. A cartoon character on fast-forward.

"What? What's going on?" I ask, but Curt doesn't answer. He's too busy being frantic.

"Shit, shit, shit, shit, shit . . ." He dumps the CDs in an empty box and trips over me as he tries to get out the door. He sets down the box, runs back in, grabs his sneakers, and puts them on as he runs back out.

I try to lift myself off the floor, but it's a slow process. I have to disentangle from the records and claw at the wall to pull myself up. My stubby fingers have no grip.

"What's wrong?" I ask again as Curt digs through the CDs like a maniac. He takes out six seemingly random ones and shoves them in my hands.

"Listen to these. A lot."

He stands still for approximately two seconds, then stashes his guitar under the piano and heads for the kitchen. My afternoon has just gone from idyllic childhood nostalgia to the wrong side of an episode of *Cops*.

"What're you doing?" I huff, my voice rising an octave. "Where are you going?"

Curt ignores me. "Yeah, sorry." He grabs a plastic Kmart bag, takes a Coke and a package of bologna from the refrigerator, and stashes them inside.

"Back door," he orders. He doesn't say it to me, but I follow anyway. I want to jump up and down, wave my huge fleshy arms, but he's busy unearthing a door to the back alley that just moments ago was blocked by the world's entire supply of used mops. Curt lets them spill all over the floor then pushes the door as far as it will go. The alley is narrow, and the space created is approximately six inches wide. I stare at it forlornly, but Curt doesn't notice because he's madly squeezing his rail-thin body through the gap. I panic.

"I won't fit," I say, huffing. "I won't fit!"

Curt pops out the other side like a watermelon emerging from the birth canal. The bologna falls out of the Kmart bag, and Curt stops for a fraction of a second to pick it up. He looks at me and grins sloppily. It's a sorry grin. A hey-better-luck-next-time grin. But it's still a grin. He turns and takes off running.

I'm left watching the exact spot where Curt disappeared. I listen to the hum of the old refrigerator and wonder what the hell just happened. The kitchen is dark, but bathed in red neon light from the living room and green neon light from the microwave clock. Ho-ho-ho. It's the Fat Kid Christmas Special.

The evidence of our invasion is strewn everywhere and I realize if someone comes back now I'm dead meat. See page two for the subway scenario. Minus the preserved leg.

I trace my steps backward, huffing as I go. The house is creepy and I have gooseflesh. Acres of it. I start toward the living room then realize my sneakers are still under the bed and have to turn back. I push my way into the miniscule bedroom, squat down, and reach my fleshy hand under someone else's bed.

My fingers close over first one sneaker, then the other. As I pull them out, the back of my hand brushes against something furry, something that feels like a severed head. *Holy shit,* I think, *it's all over. I'm going to hurl.* I leap backward, crashing into the dresser, and a thousand perfume bottles tinkle to the ground.

I put on my sneakers but don't tie them, then bolt as if my life depends on setting the world record for cross-apartment sprinting.

Imagine a rabid elephant. That's me. I pound through the living room, shaking mirrors and antique ornaments as I go. A set of glass spangles tinkle loudly, and I knock over a green vase, splashing water onto the floor. I don't stop. I head for the front door and don't breathe until my sweaty hand grasps the doorknob. The door creaks open and then . . .

Nothing. Silence. There's no one there.

I step into the brightly lit hallway looking for the distorted white mask of the serial killer from *Scream,* but there's only a discarded umbrella, two sets of mud-caked boots, and an empty bottle of Jack Daniel's. My panic subsides.

I shuffle down the hall bolstered by the light, then open the two doors to the outside. A blast of fresh air carries the scent of exhaust.

The quiet of the apartment is replaced by the sound of car horns and distant reggae. A man and woman are approaching the front door just as I exit. The man lurches forward and the woman is smoking a cigarette, digging around in her purse.

"Fuck," she says under her breath.

I pass them and the man turns around to stare.

"Holy shit, Hazel. You see that kid? That kid was, like, three hundred pounds."

The woman doesn't look up from her purse, but she sighs so loud I can hear it all the way down the street.

"Lay off the booze, Jake," she says. "Ain't no such thing as a three-hundred-pound kid."

19.

I SHOULD BE PISSED.

Curt left. He bailed. He stole stuff, made a mess, ditched me.

But he also showed me his records. And talked to me the whole day, pretending I was going to be his drummer at a real gig. He set up my daring escape.

I can't stop grinning. I sit on the subway train taking up three seats while all the straphangers glare. I ought to be hating Curt, but all I do is wonder if I'll ever see him again.

I grin all the way home and arrive approximately seven minutes before Dad will walk through the front door. Dayle is waiting in the kitchen.

"Where have you been?" he demands. He's standing in his socks and boxers cooking a half dozen eggs. Dayle's always on some special diet to gain or lose weight depending on the sports season. When it's football season he has to gain weight, so he eats obsessively, but when it's wrestling season he has to lose it all to wrestle in the lower weight class, so he lives for weeks on a carrot and a glass of water. It's fall, so he's trying to gain. The eggs sizzle in the pan and my stomach rumbles.

"What do you care?" I snarl. But I'm hoping he'll give me one of his eggs. "I was with Curt. Practicing. Hey, can I have one of those?"

Dayle makes a face; the funny kind he used to make when we were kids. Back when he just pretended to be annoyed with me. I think that means he's going to give me one, but he doesn't.

"Get your own," he says.

I reach for a donut instead.

"You skipped the whole day, you know," Dayle adds, as if he's informing me of something. "I could totally tell Dad. Do you have any idea how embarrassing it was to have my senior sumo brother seen in public with that psycho guitar player?"

I pause with the donut halfway to my mouth. Immediately, I sense that something has changed. Curt has progressed from homeless trash to a psycho guitar player. And Dayle is trying to converse with me.

I put the donut down, and grab a plate and fork from the dish drainer. I stab one of his eggs and slide it onto my plate. "He *is* a psycho guitar player," I say. "In fact, we almost got arrested today for breaking and entering . . . but I'm sure you wouldn't want to hear about that."

Dayle glares at me and I smile. I turn and carry my plate into the living room, grabbing the donut on my way out. *Fuck you,* I think, trying to stifle a grin.

FAT KID RULES THE WORLD.

20.

THURSDAY, A GIRL INTENTIONALLY speaks to me for the first time. She stands next to me with her silky legs crossed, holding her books to her chest. She says, "So, do you really know Curt MacCrae?"

I should say, "No—who the hell does?" but instead I say, "Yeah. We've got a band."

She giggles. The books slide and I try not to stare at her chest.

"I saw Curt play with Smack Metal Puppets once. He's really good. Is it true he's, like, twenty-one?"

I don't know the answer, but I nod as if I do. She bites her lip.

"My friend thinks Curt will be on MTV someday. I said he wouldn't sell out like that but she said it wouldn't be selling out if he kept the intensity of his music. He's real . . . authentic. You know?"

I do know. I also know there's a response expected of me, but I can't imagine what it is. I can't talk because I'm terrified I'll huff and she'll laugh. I say nothing.

"Well, see you around," she says.

"Yeah," I say, watching her slide away from me. "See you around."

21.

THE NEXT TIME I SEE CURT it's by accident. I'm walking to the F train at Washington Square, daydreaming about the girl in the cafeteria, wondering if by any chance Dayle saw her talking to me. It's Saturday and I'm coming back from a dentist appointment.

I'm happy because I'm thinking about the girl, but I'm bummed because Dayle was supposed to go to the dentist, too, but he wouldn't. No big deal. Except I keep remembering how it was after Mom got sick when he was too little to ride the subway by himself. I'd hold his hand and put his token in the slot like a real big brother. That was a long time ago, before I caused him mortal embarrassment. Before he turned into a self-centered asshole.

We don't talk about it, *ever,* but when Mom was dying and Dad had to spend all his time at the hospital, it was me and Dayle. Buddies. Pals. I swear to God he looked up to me. I don't have any proof, but I remember the way he'd follow me around the apartment and try to get me to play basketball at the park. I was never good at sports, even when I was thin, but in those days I could still make it to the court and back.

Now Dad plays basketball with Dayle. Twice a week. And I invite him to the dentist's office. *No wonder he hates me. . . .*

Still, he could've come.

The whole thing makes me tired and I wish there were someplace to sit down. My flesh moves like silicone weights around my waist, arms, and legs, and I feel people's eyes boring into me. I feel my body growing larger as they stare and can't help thinking about the last time I went anywhere with Dayle. That was last week, right before I met Curt. We were walking together and Dayle was pissed because he had to walk really slowly. *As if that's a crime . . .* Then there was this group of kids near the stairs.

I mentally rewrite the whole scene. Next time, when they laughed, I wouldn't let them laugh at Dayle, too. I'd say something. I'd defend us. . . . I'd say, "Fuck off, morons." Or else maybe I'd say, "Get a life." No, wait. Those sound stupid. I try to think what a punk rock drummer would say.

I'm about to come up with the perfect retort when I hear this amazing voice filling the underground passage. There's a guitar grinding away and the voice is deep and tortured, filled with a rage that sounds real yet amazingly melodic. There's something raw and familiar about it. Something I recognize. I round the corner and shuffle faster.

Sure enough. There he is.

Curt's got his amp plugged into the floor socket and he's intent on his guitar. He looks small and pale behind it, but he's got a large crowd standing around listening. More people stop as he breaks into a cross between a wail and a shout and the guitar crescendos like a siren. It's a primitive blending. Makes me think of wild animal orgies.

I try to listen for the things Curt told me about music. I hear some of them—the way the chords and the chorus don't quite fit, and the rhythms sound angular and unbalanced. It's intense, almost obscene, but women in power suits and men in horn-rimmed glasses are clapping enthusiastically, throwing money into the waiting bucket. Curt doesn't thank them. He doesn't even acknowledge them—just leans down and scoops out their dollar bills.

I stand there, a mute idiot agonizing over whether to speak. I decide I won't say anything because I don't want him to think I searched him out. *Good decision, right?* Don't want him to think I need anything more than he's already given me.

Curt sees me right away.

"Big T!" He's about to start another song but stops and unplugs his guitar. Just like that. He picks up the bucket and shoves his amp awkwardly inside. Apparently, the show's over. Moms with strollers and little old men linger, confused, before dispersing.

"Hey," Curt says, jogging up to me. "I've been, you know, looking for you."

Of course it's a lie but the tips of my ears turn red anyway. Curt hands me the bucket and amp. "Carry this for me?" He flips his guitar onto his back while I glance around hoping everyone sees that I'm now carrying Curt's amp. They don't seem to care.

"You were good," I say at last. Curt grins.

"Wait until we get your drum part in there, man. Oooh, yeah. Couldn't you hear it? I hear it in my head . . . when I'm playing. You'll be perfect, T. Perfect."

He's hyper today, dancing ahead of me, running back to let me catch up. A kid without his Ritalin. I wonder where we're going.

"Curt," I say at last. "I'm not so sure I can really, actually, well, *play* the drums." I lick my teeth.

Curt misses a beat, but only one. His smile returns like a boomerang.

"No way, man," he breathes. "All you gotta do is hit 'em hard. That's all you gotta do."

I want to argue. If I wasn't such a pathetic stooge I *would* argue, but Curt keeps nodding to himself, so I let him. I shuffle along, grinning a clandestine grin while Curt darts ahead, a denizen ferret of the underground, huge black guitar slung over his shoulder.

22.

WE END UP AT MY apartment building. Curt's suggestion.

Actually, he gets on the subway with me and follows me all the way home. We're secret agents on the same mission, both pretending we don't know where we're going. DOUBLE-O FAT KID AND CURT POWERS. Minus the chicks. Every woman who gets on the subway migrates quickly to the opposite end.

We get out at the Second Avenue station, then walk to my apartment. It's not far, but Curt has to walk real slow in order to pretend he's not following me and I can tell it's hard for him. After a while he gives up and walks ahead of me.

I hesitate when we reach the front steps, but Curt doesn't. He waits for me to unlock the security door, then walks right inside like he belongs there. I've lived here seventeen years and still can't do that. Curt even nods at my downstairs neighbor who's standing in the hallway. She nods back but stares at me with disgust. *Skinny old hag* . . . I ignore her and carry the amp up the stairs.

I'm soaked in sweat when we get to the top. I'm breathing heavy and my T-shirt is clinging to my chest. Curt takes the bucket back while I open the door with my key. He slips inside as soon as the door is open, looks around, and nods in satisfaction at the empty apartment. I double over, catching my breath.

Curt doesn't wait. He moves straight toward my room, takes off his guitar, props it against the wall, then pretends to be scanning my stuff while really he searches for his CDs. I watch from the hallway as he spots them on the floor next to my mattress, scoops them up, and drops them in his bucket. He looks relieved, then sheepish.

"You have got to . . . I mean, really you should do something about this room," he says. "You've got nothing up here. No Big T trinkage or any such sort of thing. Where are the band posters? Where's the graffiti?" He frowns disapprovingly, then turns his gaze to me. "And you *must* spice up those clothes, man. Not for the sake of spiciness per se, but simply because they're not you. There's no Big T in your big Ts."

He's cracked himself up and I stop long enough to stare at what I'm wearing. Bland tan pants. A T-shirt that reads DOG DAYS OF SUMMER.

"There's not much in my size—" I start, but Curt interrupts.

"Screw that," he says. "You make your size. You make your walls. It's not about what's out there."

Then what's it about? I almost ask. But deep down I hope I already know.

Curt shakes his head. "Listen, man, I gotta take a nap, maybe eat something. Very important. While I'm doing that you could work on this a bit, huh?"

He says it as if I've been shirking an important duty out of sheer laziness, then slips off his sneakers and curls up on my mattress. I'm glad I made my bed this morning because he's filthy again, but I can't tell him to move. He's just made my life. Besides, I'm too busy staring at my room wondering what the hell I could possibly plaster on my walls.

23.

CURT SLEEPS FOR HOURS and I start to worry that he's sick or something. I worry about it in a distracted sort of way because really I'm trying hard to come up with ideas. *Interior decorator, I am not.*

I walk into Dayle's room and stare at his sports posters and team banners. It pisses me off that I have nothing to show for my life. If it's all about what's inside, like Curt says, then how come Dayle has everything? I should have something, shouldn't I? Something resembling raw meat or splattered Fat Kid?

I go back in my room and dig around under my bed, but all I find is an old *Saturday Night Live* poster covered in dust balls. My shuffling wakes up Curt. He sits up with his eyes closed, then opens them and squints. It's getting dark, so the room is dim and it takes him a moment to orient to his surroundings. I expect him to be disappointed, but he seems excited to find himself at my house.

"Oh, yeah," he says, low under his breath. He glances at the *Saturday Night Live* poster and nods approvingly.

"What else?"

I shrug. "I don't think I have anything else," I say defensively. Curt's eyes narrow.

"Everybody's got something," he mutters. "Here, put this CD on." He crawls over to the bucket and takes out a CD. I put it on my stereo and crank it until he nods. The drumbeat is in-your-face relentless and it makes me want to move.

"All right then."

Curt scans my room. He opens my closet, then my dresser and digs through both. He pulls out an old tartan blanket, my sneakers, a pair of tan pants, last week's comic section, a black marker, my box of photos, a bottle of glue. . . . Midway through he pauses and asks if I've got something to eat. I pull a box of food from under my bed. He nods in satisfaction, and the work begins.

We work steady for a long time, and for once in my life I forget that I'm fat. I don't entirely forget, but I mostly forget. And when I remember it's because Curt is working it into a mural on my wall. He draws caricatures of naked women on my tan pants, then tacks them up along with every candy wrapper and box we empty. They make a giant trail exploding out of my pants. FAT KID DIARRHEA.

It's my idea to tack the shoes to the ceiling. They're sneakers Dad bought me for gym. I stuff them with Ho Hos and use red licorice in place of shoelaces. We cut up last week's comic strips and glue them into a big square around the *Saturday Night Live* poster. It looks funky and I stare at it for five minutes while Curt digs through my photo box.

"Which of these do you want up, man?" he keeps asking. This one? *This one?* He's pulling out pictures of Dad and Mom. One of Dayle and me wearing matching baseball caps, arms draped around each other's shoulders. It's one of my favorites. Curt puts it down and takes out an eight-by-ten of Dad in uniform and says I should put it on the door. Suggests I blow it up poster size. I can tell he really likes it, but I shake my head.

"No pictures," I say. It's the first idea of Curt's I've disagreed with. I want to agree, but I don't think I can stand having the family we once were staring at me every day. Mom before Cancer, Dad before Retirement, me before Fat, and Dayle before . . . I look hard at the picture of Dayle. Dayle before *what?*

Curt shoves the loose pictures back in the box, but he takes the photo of Dad and slips it inside his shirt when he thinks I'm not looking. "Okay," he says, "but the drum set goes over there."

He points to a corner of my room and I try to imagine a drum set in that spot. I'm thinking I could handle that, and I'm just about to say as much when the front door creaks and Dad's and Dayle's voices drift down the hall. Suddenly Curt's standing up, gathering his things.

"Seeing as there are plans and such, you know, or I'd stay, except for how it is." Curt pushes his hair away from his face while his eyes dart about the room. They linger on my last candy bar.

"Want it?" I ask, but Curt shakes his head.

"Can't," he says emphatically. He takes a chewable Imodium out of his pocket, licks it, and tries to stick it to my mirror.

"Looks good in here. Gots personality now." He stares happily at the walls and ceiling. Then we hear footsteps coming down the hall.

"Yeah. So. Meet you on Monday. We've got to, you know, *conceptualize.*" He doesn't wait for my reply, just nods to himself as if it's all agreed, and picks up his stuff. He's got the guitar on his back and the amp in the bucket and I wonder where the hell he's going with all that stuff. I would ask, but at that moment Dad and Dayle are passing in the hallway and Curt scuttles past, a spastic blur mumbling incoherently, laden down with all his worldly goods.

I stare after him, thinking I should follow, but Dayle stops outside my door, buried in Gap bags and Abercrombie & Fitch boxes. He peers at me with disdain. I'm hoping he'll say something about my room, but he doesn't.

"Dad," he says, "can't you tell Troy not to let that . . . that . . . *sewer rat* into the house? He smells like shit and we all know he's a junkie." He turns to me. "What, are you on drugs now? That's all I need."

My father stops midstride. He's wearing his usual khaki pants and navy blue T-shirt—the general-on-his-day-off clothes. He glances at Dayle and clears his throat.

"Troy," he says, "you are aware that your friend is a junkie, are you not?"

I shouldn't be startled, but I am. A surge of adrenaline rushes through my body and the small hairs on the back of my neck rise.

"He's not . . . ," I begin.

My father's eyes narrow.

"Troy," Dad says. "Curt's a textbook case. Classic symptoms. I've seen junkies and your friend is definitely one of them. He needs to clean himself up. Take charge of his life."

I've heard that phrase uttered with every possible inflection in every possible setting. "Take charge" over easy. Scrambled with hash browns. One "take charge" with ketchup and weenies. Dayle has a small, satisfied smirk on his face as my father's voice continues to drone.

"Now, I don't mind giving him a place to shower, some clean clothes, a hot meal," Dad's saying, "people deserve a decent leg up, and I know they can change if they set their minds to it. All it takes is perseverance. But Curt's got to take advantage of those opportunities. Understand?"

Of course I understand. It goes unsaid that I, Troy Billings, understand.

My father looks down at me.

"You understand what I'm telling you, Troy? I'm glad you have a friend, but don't get too attached. . . ."

My gut churns. I think of all the opportunities my father has given me that I've failed to take advantage of. I make a mental list. Two gym memberships paid in full, a complete weight set given to me for Christmas, eighteen sessions with two different psychologists, a year and a half with a nutritionist, eleven diet books, two healthy-eating videos, a free consultation with a personal trainer, two summers at fat camp, and nearly perfect, healthy genes.

My father waits for my response.

"I don't think he is . . . ," I huff, but my body's inflating beyond my control. I start to stutter. "I-I've got to see Curt be-because of the band. For practice . . ."

Dayle snorts.

"You're hyperventilating," he says with a laugh. It's true. I am. But I wonder why that's funny.

24.

IRRESPONSIBLE FAT KID WAITS FOR JUNKIE FRIEND.

Monday, I linger at the basketball court having imaginary conversations with Dad and Dayle in which I gain the upper hand every single time. I use words like "loyalty" and "tolerance" in a sweeping, grandiose manner and they cower. Hee-hee.

Except, this time Curt doesn't show up. At all. I stand there waiting, scanning each person who walks past the chain-link fence, but Curt is not one of them. The fourth period bell rings and I know I should go back inside—*know I should*—but I think, *Fat Kid Screws Up*

Again, and my legs refuse to move. I meet the eyes of a passing businessman and he looks away, studiously adjusting the antenna on his cell phone. I stare at the brick facade of the school but cannot drag myself into its gaping maw.

I decide there's been a mistake. A huge, vast mistake.

I set out for the subway without thinking about it. My feet slog forward, pulling my weight along with them. I wait for the F train, convinced I'll get off at Second Avenue and go home. But I don't get off.

I sit next to the door, unmoving, while skinny people enter and exit. Their eyes are careful not to hover, but I can tell what they're thinking—MUTANT TEENAGER UNFIT FOR PUBLIC SCHOOL: DEVIANT FAT KID WITH NOWHERE TO GO.

I get off at Curt's stop, East Broadway, and head in the direction we walked last week. I can't remember which street he lives on, but I know his place was near the bridge. I walk past a park and a jumble of markets, past the low-income housing complexes. Everything looks wrong and I can't tell if it's because I'm going the wrong way or because everything *is* wrong. I've simultaneously managed to convince myself that Curt is expecting me and that he never really existed in the first place. I say it doesn't matter, but I'm a big fat liar. I shuffle urgently and start to sweat.

I almost miss Curt's place, but at the last minute I recognize the AN IQUES sign in the window. I stand directly in front of the cement steps and stare between the security bars. Now that I'm here, this doesn't seem like such a great idea.

I imagine Curt, somewhere inside, hiding his skinny body in some angle or crevice. He's probably avoiding me, but I can't get past the idea that maybe, *just maybe,* he meant for me to meet him and he's waiting for me to show up. Waiting to form a punk rock band.

My hand reaches for the knob. It should be locked, so when it pushes open my heart races. *Is it open for me?*

I take two steps forward and face the inner door. The apartment's mailboxes are right beside me. Johnson. Gonzales. A smudge. I take a deep breath and reach forward. The door pushes open, and I let my breath wheeze out. *Shhzzzhhsshh.*

It's true, I think. *It's Monday and he's here, waiting to practice. . . .* I smile and walk toward apartment number one.

I push open the door, the green one with the peeling paint. It's partly ajar, and inside I can see the edge of the piano. I take a step forward and that's when I see the man standing in the living room.

Just like that, I'm the lead in a bad horror movie.

"Who are you?" he bellows. *"Who* are *you?!"*

The man's greasy black hair is matted to his head and his face is unshaven, days' worth of stubble protruding from pockmarked skin. I recognize him. He's wearing the same coffee-stained T-shirt and brown dungarees he was wearing last week. I freeze.

"I'm Troy," I stammer. "I'm . . . I'm . . . I'm Troy. I'm looking for Curt." It comes out in a stream of saliva.

The man uses both hands to steady himself against the piano. His face contorts like Silly Putty and his eyes dance as if they have a life of their own.

"Who the fuck are you? Where's Curt?" he demands. "You come here to meet that sorry-ass son of a . . ." The line of epithets continues while my brain screams, *Get out, get out, get out.* But I can't move.

"No . . ." Huff. "No . . . I didn't say that. . . ." Huff.

The man snarls and steps forward. "You tell Curt he comes around here one more time and I'll shoot him. You tell 'im I know he's been sneaking in here stealing my bologna." His eyes narrow.

"Where is he?" The voice is a hiss and he hunkers down low, trying to sneak a look past me. "Did he send you here? Is he in the hall? He tell you to come here and steal my food? I swear I'll tear your goddamn, fucking balls off. . . ."

My body releases like a spring. I turn and bolt, and hear the man crashing behind me. I make it to the first door, then the second, down the steps, and onto the street. Behind me, the man slithers to the doorway and screams after me. He's calling me a "fat ass, tub of lard, shit-brained motherfucker" but I don't stop to argue. He's probably right, but at least I've got my balls.

25.

I'M BACK INSIDE THE SCHOOL building. Back to the glorious confines of familiar misery.

EXULTANT FAT KID REJOICES.

I've never been so willing to go to class. I run through the halls— at least, I come as close to running as I can get. I slide in short bursts, then slow to a panting crawl. I'm sweating like a gallon tub of ice in the Amazon, pulling my T-shirt away from my chest to fan away the sweat, then wiping my vast, greasy forehead with my sleeve. All I can think about is returning to class. *Must resume normal day. Must pretend nothing happened.*

That's when I see Curt sitting by my locker.

I stare in disbelief.

"Hey, you're late," he says when he sees me. He's obviously picked my lock and now he's seemingly preoccupied by leafing through my textbooks. "This stupid guy, um, a teacher-guy maybe . . . came by and asked for my hall pass and I told him . . ." A bunch of papers spill out and Curt wisks them into a pile. "I told him I got kicked out of that class over there for being rude." He points at the door across the hall with his chin and laughs. "I told him I was sitting here thinking about being more polite next time. Hell . . . Hey, man. What's up with you? You're late for practice."

I am the walrus, perched atop a muddy slope when the bank caves in below him. The world washes away like so much mud.

"I almost got killed," I pant. "I went to your . . . house . . . and . . ." I pause because Curt is now eating the Twinkies I had stashed in my locker. I take a deep breath and start again.

"I was at your house. I *went* to your house." I wait for the reaction, but Curt keeps eating the Twinkies. He eats each bite very carefully, licking out all the cream before eating the cake. I'm distracted.

"There was . . . this guy there, and . . ."

Curt looks up, interested for the first time. "The asshole?"

I nod, catch my breath, and force my cheeks not to puff. I have to end the lie, and it *must . . . not . . . be . . . funny.*

"I can't be in a band with you," I huff. It comes out in a mudslide of a confession. "I can't play the drums; you need to get someone else. It was all just a lie, you know? Just a shallow, pathetic lie . . ."

Curt's brow furrows, and he looks up and down the hall as if I'm talking to someone else.

"T, man, chill," he says. But I can't chill. Chilling is not within my fat, sweaty grasp.

"I can't play the drums!" I yell, much louder than I intend.

Curt laughs.

"Wow," he says. He finishes the last bite of my Twinkie and licks his fingers as I stand there twitching.

"That was kind of funny."

He waits a minute.

"So, are you ready for practice?"

I would strangle him if I could. I really would.

Curt grins, stands up, punches me in the arm, hops three times. Yawns.

"What?" he says when I don't respond. "What? So you went to my house and the asshole probably said he was going to kill me if I steal anything else . . . blah, blah, blah. He always says that. Bad refrain. You can't listen to people like that." Curt bends down to tie his sneaker, which is perpetually untied.

"Besides," he adds, speaking to the floor, "you could've taken him, easy. You could've reached out and squashed him. Sat on him if you wanted to."

Curt finds this hysterical. He proceeds to demonstrate how I could have sat on his stepfather. The demonstration involves making his butt look very big, then running in a half circle to play the role of terrified stepfather watching my huge ass descend.

I stop twitching and chuckle despite myself. I'm trying hard not to, but can't help it. *Goddamn him, it's funny.*

"Let's go, then," Curt says, dusting himself off. I give up and follow him back out the door.

I ask him to tell me where we're going, but he refuses to answer. Tells me something about old friends, the space-time continuum, and matters of utmost importance. I'm guessing he doesn't know. We leave the school building and head toward the subway.

"Curt," I say after a while. "You really think I could've taken your stepfather? Beat him up, I mean?"

Curt scowls.

"You make it sound like the 1950s."

I wonder. *Were there obese teenage freaks in the 1950s?* I don't say anything and Curt sighs.

"Yeah," he says at last. "Yeah, already. You most definitely, without a doubt could've taken my stepfather. You, T," he adds, "are The Man."

I mean to correct him. *No, I'm the Fat Kid,* but I don't.

26.

WE REACH THE STATION and I follow Curt down the dank steps, avoiding pools of mysterious liquid that collect in the corners of the staircase. I'm walking in a zone, hung up on the admission that I could've won a fair fight. *It's true, see?* That's the beauty of it. As soon as he said it I knew it was true, only it had never occurred to me before. Years of torment over imaginary losses now seem like such a waste.

Curt cases the station while I waddle slowly, mentally erasing thousands of predicted pummelings. When I finally reach the turnstiles Curt slides up next to me and gives me a signal. It's a strange, skinny-person's hand motion and I stare blankly until I realize what he wants. He wants to jump the turnstile and thinks that if I swipe my Metrocard very slowly while he hops across I'll block the view of the unsuspecting clerk who's watching from the booth. That way I pay, Curt doesn't, and the New York transit system is none the wiser. Unless, of course, the clerk catches on and calls the cops. Then we'll be cleaning gutters for the next month. A surge of fear pulses through my body. Then I stop. *Hell.* I swipe my card.

Curt jumps and we're clear.

He lands in a hop on the other side. "Did you see that?" he says. "Oh, man, that was the coolest! That was so fucking awesome! Do you know how many trains I could ride for free? We could do this all the time. We could sell your services. . . ." He stops hopping and wipes his brow. "What's ironic," he adds, shaking his head, "is that everyone's so busy trying not to look like they're looking at you that they're really not looking at you."

He says it so confused I almost don't understand. Then I look up.

"Wait. So what you're saying . . ." I pause. "What you're saying is . . . people aren't really looking at me?"

Curt's eyes flash and for the first time all day he stops moving. There's something there that isn't respect, and isn't sympathy, but hints at everything I don't yet know. He leans forward.

"Exactly."

27.

FAT KID CONTEMPLATES QUANTUM PHYSICS.

If the universe is, in fact, curved when before we thought it was flat . . .

I consider what's just been said. If Curt's observation is true, then it's possible, though not probable, that people are not always looking at me when I think they're looking at me.

Matter begins to bend unpredictably.

If people are not always looking at me, then the eye rays that make me bloat to the size of a blue whale whenever I'm in public are perhaps more diluted than I think they are.

Time speeds up as the rate of expanding particles increases.

Perhaps I am merely a sperm whale after all.

The scientific community has been shaken. Truly shaken.

28.

I FOLLOW CURT BLINDLY, not watching where we're going. I don't care. The world has changed. I'm a born-again fat kid ready to drape myself in a choir robe and sing the "Hallelujah" chorus.

We arrive at our destination—the place called The Dump—just after two o'clock. Curt lets us in the rickety, old back door and I burst in ready for anything. It's empty and smells like dust. Most of the furniture is broken or newly repaired, but there's a huge stage up front with a drum set, two guitars, and a microphone stand on it.

"Whose instruments are those? Is that your guitar? Who're we waiting for?"

I'm trying not to be annoying, but finally, Curt sits at the bar and puts his head down. Just as I get excited, he gets tired.

"I'm hungry," he moans. "My stomach hurts." His voice is low and it's almost like he isn't saying it to me. I shift in my chair, noticing he looks a little pale.

"You got any money?" he asks. His cheek is squished against the wood, so the words come out mashed.

"I've got a five," I say. Curt perks up, watches me closely. He doesn't say a word, but his eyes light up.

"McDonald's?" I ask at last.

Curt shrugs. "Yup. Okay." He's nonchalant, but says it very quickly. "What do you want?" he asks. I answer without thinking.

"Quarter Pounder with cheese."

I can see Curt calculating in his mind. A Quarter Pounder with cheese is almost three dollars.

"Make that a hamburger," I say. "Just a plain hamburger."

Curt smiles and tells me he'll be right back. I grin, believing him. *Poor Oblivious Fat Kid.*

29.

HOURS HAVE PASSED. World civilizations have risen and collapsed. Seasons have changed. Government regimes have been deposed. No Curt. No hamburger.

I'm just about to get up and leave when the creaky door eeks open and an awkward scarecrow of a guy with a purple Mohawk walks through. I stand stiffly and huff when he sees me, as if I'm guilty of sitting where I don't belong. The guy stops walking and looks confused. He looks around the room as if there's *got* to be someone else here. He has one eyebrow pierced with a safety pin and a thousand tattoos on each arm. His black T-shirt reads WHITE NOISE. He looks vaguely familiar, and I realize he's the drummer for Smack Metal Puppets. Ollie Oliver.

"I'm looking for Curt," he says at last. His voice cracks as if it only just recently changed, but he's older than me, so I figure that's just the way he talks. I release a puff of air, and try not to say anything stupid.

"He went . . . for McDonald's."

Stupid. I cringe. I sound like Chris Farley in *Tommy Boy.* Ollie studies me, summing me up. His mouth moves to one side, then the other.

"Well . . . I'm supposed to meet some drummer here for lessons."

"Uh, yeah. That's probably me," I say. "Except Curt didn't say anything about . . ."

He circles me in long, measured strides. He's got a pointy face and a large beak of a nose and he leans back at the hips when he walks.

"No offense," he says, voice rising, "but how old are you?"

It wasn't the question I was expecting.

"Seventeen," I say. "I graduate this year."

Ollie runs his fingers over his scalp and scowls. He plays with one of his rings—a golden skull and crossbones. Scowls again.

"And you've played drums before?"

I nod, then pause. "In junior high," I offer. My stomach jiggles. "Until seventh grade . . ."

He squints and I wait for him to laugh. He doesn't laugh.

"You're kidding. Please tell me you're kidding."

I shake my head.

"That fucker." He punches his palm with his fist and I panic. "Listen, you don't have to . . . I mean, I don't really . . ."

Ollie raises one tattooed hand. Dragons loop around his fingers. "A deal's a deal," he says, breathing long and deep. "I should've known, is all. It's my own damn fault. Curt said he'd found a drummer who just needed a few lessons to get ready for next month's gig. I assumed . . . Ah, *hell.*"

His voice drops on "hell."

"Well," he says, "do you want to play the drums, or what?"

I nod stupidly. So far, as near as I can tell, Ollie Oliver is disconcertingly . . . nice. Throws me off guard.

He leads me on stage and I stand behind the drum set pretending I'm actually going to have a lesson. It's surreal, as if I've drifted out of my life and can't get back in. I look around thinking, *Where am I? Where's Curt? What's happening?* I'm nervous and sweaty and it takes me a long time to sit down. I keep imagining how my butt will spill over the sides of the little drum stool. Ollie informs me that the stool is called a throne and that makes it even worse. Sounds like a toilet. Makes me feel like there's something obscene about sitting down.

Ollie's patient, though. He waits while I reposition numerous times. He drags a chair across the old wooden floor then heaves it on stage and climbs up after it in an uncoordinated way. He sits down beside me and his long legs stretch a mile in front of him.

"So, you're the drummer," he says, almost to himself. "Hmm," he comments.

I silently agree. It's as good a commentary on my predicament as anything I've heard yet.

"You like the drums?" Ollie asks at last.

It's a crucial question, so I lie.

"Oh, yeah. Yeah." Pause. "Curt and I are going to form this band, see—" Ollie cuts me off with the wave of one tattooed hand.

"Mmm. Curt told me all that," he says. "Rage/Tectonic. Good name. He told me your first gig's in five *weeks*." His voice goes up on "weeks" and he chuckles. "Quick turnaround. Typical Curt."

I think, *Where is Curt?* and stare at the door like a dog who has to go out.

"Erm," I say.

Ollie agrees. "Got your work cut out for you, don't ya? Of course, it's totally doable," he amends. "Five weeks is plenty of time and if anyone can do it, Curt can."

I look at my shoe and Ollie sighs.

"Well," he comments, astutely. "I meant, *you* can." Silence stretches like taffy. "So, anyway . . . we might as well start at the beginning."

Yes, I think, *might as well.*

Ollie sighs again. "This," he says at last, "is a drum set. . . ."

Ollie starts explaining stuff about drums, telling me great details about the components of a drum set and how to take care of them. He talks about the history of rock and names the most respected drummers past and present. I imagine most of it is pretty interesting, but I wouldn't know because I can't comprehend a word he's saying. I keep staring at the door thinking, *Where is Curt with my hamburger?*

He finally shows up just as Ollie starts "refreshing" me on basic rhythms. Curt skulks in like a kid sneaking home after a late-night joy ride. He slides through the creaky door, darts to the bar, cleans a stray glass with his sleeve as if he's been standing there for hours, sits in the audience, then finally makes his way on stage. His hands are empty and he has ketchup stains on his shirt. No hamburger. I almost leap over the drum set and squash him. I think about my newfound knowledge and am confident I could squash Curt with little effort. But Curt's oblivious to my power. He grins at Ollie, then at me.

"Great, man. This is great," he says in a rush. "You sound great."

I haven't actually hit the drums yet.

Ollie claps Curt on the shoulder and grins. It's a weird grin because I can tell he's trying not to do it. He looks like he wants to be mad, but isn't.

"Insane freak," Ollie says. "What the hell are you up to? Troy can't play the drums, you know. . . ."

I've been trying to say this ever since I met Curt, but now I'm insulted. Curt just shrugs.

"Hey," he says, hopping twice, "teach him that cool rim thing. . . ."

30.

QUESTIONS ON THE AGENDA: *What is Curt thinking?! Why is he pretending I am going to be a drummer in his band? How do I get out of this without ruining my life? Can I pretend to play a gig? What is Curt thinking?!*

I sit on stage, a massive silhouette, playing rhythms as they're dictated to me. I think, *Why am I doing this?* and flail miserably. I've crossed a line somewhere and can't figure out how that happened. Without meaning to I've overstepped that yellow line, only this time my body is flying through the air and the F train's coming.

Curt sits backward on a wooden chair while Ollie reminds me to keep the bass drum going while I add the other drum parts. We've been working on the same patterns for the last hour and I'm tired. My arms ache and my legs hurt. I want to go home. I keep thinking about the middle part of my day. The part where I felt assertive and slightly less bloated, not the part where I almost got killed. My mind wanders and I lose the beat.

"No, man," Ollie says. "You'd have it if you'd concentrate."

I shake my head. "I don't think—" I start, but Curt interrupts.

"Don't try so hard," he tells me. "You're just starting, so don't worry about what you sound like."

It's the most absurd thing I've ever heard. *Who was worried about that?* I'm worried about looking like the Goodyear Drummer. I'm worried about potentially eternal humiliation. I'm worried about being manipulated into something I absolutely, positively, no-way-in-hell can do. My stomach growls loudly.

"I can't concentrate," I mutter. "I have to get home. Dad's going to freak."

Ollie and Curt exchange glances—horrible, sarcastic, we-knew-it-all-along glances. Skinny-people-in-cahoots glances. *I hate them.* I dig my fat heels into the floor.

"I've got to go home," I say, firmly. "This has been fun and all, but there's no way I'm playing a gig. I can't play in front of people. I hyperventilate. I can't . . . do it. I know I've said this before, but this time I *mean it.*"

It's the most assertive speech I've ever made, which would be gratifying except for the fact that Ollie looks at Curt and Curt looks at Ollie and they both pretend to be clueless. They're playing the we-can't-see-that-you're-fat card and I *hate* that.

Curt stares intently at a loose floorboard while Ollie studies the graffiti on the wall.

"Fine," I say, turning to Curt. "Ignore me all you want, but I'm still not doing it. Trust me, it's for the best. Find another drummer. Find *anyone else.*" *Someone normal,* I think. *Someone skinny.* I plead with him in my brain. *Listen to me. Just this once, listen to me. . . .*

Curt and Ollie glance at each other, then Curt nods.

"Okay," he says at last. I wait for more, then pause, confused. "Okay?"

Curt shrugs. "Yup. Okay." He gets up and slides his chair back in place. Ollie unknots his long legs.

"You still owe Smack Metal Puppets a gig," he says to Curt, "for today's lesson. Saturday night . . ."

Curt nods. "Right. Saturday."

They're moving on as if nothing happened while I sit like a wart on the nose of the drum set. Ollie turns to me.

"If you change your mind . . . ," he says. I blink rapidly, then stutter my response.

"I . . . no, I mean, I won't." It seems like the right thing to say after an assertive speech, but now I'm not so sure. I stand up really slowly. Suddenly, I don't want to leave.

31.

I THINK I'VE MADE a huge mistake. A Fat Kid–sized mistake. I don't know it yet, but actually, I've made two of them.

I arrive home exhausted, hungry, and sweating and all I want to do is eat. Then I see my father waiting in the kitchen. He stands by the sink, so stiff he's a two-by-four. Dayle's standing there, too, but he smiles smugly and disappears when he sees me.

"School called," Dad says.

"They did?" I'd forgotten all about school. My father nods and indicates a kitchen chair.

"Sit down," he orders. I sit facing the kitchen table and he turns on the overhead light. The rest of the house is dim, so the light seems too bright. I place my sweaty hands flat against the tabletop, gripping the edge. Dad wastes no time.

"Where were you today?" he asks.

I puff. "I went to Curt's house to practice, then to this place called The Dump."

"Did you use drugs?"

"No . . ."

Dad leans forward. His breath smells like stale coffee.

"Did Curt use drugs?"

I shake my head and my cheeks flap. "No," I say, imagining the torture that will come if I withhold information. "Curt wasn't even there at first. When I went to his house only his stepfather was home."

I wait for Dad to ask if Curt's stepfather used drugs, but he doesn't. "What did you do there?" he barks.

The stress of the day is too much. FAT KID CRACKS UNDER PRESSURE. I start from the beginning, spilling every last humiliating detail.

"Curt's stepfather was a real creep, and I almost got killed, and I know I shouldn't've been there but we were supposed to practice and I thought Curt would be home, you know, like he was last week, except he wasn't, and his stepfather was drunk and he kept saying he was going to kill Curt if he stole any more bologna and he thought I knew where Curt was so he got really mad, and then I ran and I thought he would follow me but he didn't, and then I got to my locker and I was going to go back to class, honest, but Curt was there and

70

he said he thought I could've taken his stepfather . . . you know, in a fight or something, and then he said we needed to practice, so we went to this place called The Dump—"

Dad puts his fingers on his temples and closes his eyes.

"Enough . . . enough!" He has to say it twice before I finally shut up. He looks like he might go insane, and finally he abandons his military stance and slumps down at the kitchen table. The Disappointed Dysfunctional Parent sign flashes wildly above his head and he looks up at me with tired eyes.

"Curt's stepfather threatened you?" he asks.

I pause, surprised. "Yes," I say at last. My father's jaw tightens.

"And he threatened Curt?" he asks.

I nod slowly.

"And Curt said you could've defended yourself?"

I mean to look contrite, but grin sheepishly. Dad makes a pained wheezing sound.

"And you've skipped school before to practice with Curt?" he asks.

I nod again. "Just once," I offer. "Just once to listen to CDs. Well, er . . . we sort of had to practice this week because Curt agreed to play some gigs with this band if the drummer would give me lessons. But it's over, Dad. Don't worry. It's *sooo* over."

Dad is quiet for a long time and I start to feel really guilty. When he finally says something, his voice is low and tired. "Troy," he says at last. "What didn't I give you? Haven't I been a good father? What didn't I . . .?" He can't finish the sentence.

I shut my eyes.

"Dad," I whisper, "it's really over. I swear. I told Curt to forget the whole idea. I know I can't play the drums. It was a stupid lie in the first place. It won't happen again."

My father shakes his head. "See that it doesn't," he says. He looks like he wants to say something else, but he pushes away from the table and stands up. He looks at me one last time, then turns and leaves the kitchen.

32.

MY BRIEF, IMAGINARY CAREER as a punk rock drummer is now officially over.

The next day I arrive home with the front of my favorite T-shirt plastered to my chest. It's stained with tomato sauce from when I was tripped at lunch. I landed in the exact center of my lunch tray and the entire cafeteria found it hysterical, so I had to concede there must have been humor in it. Dayle laughed the loudest and the longest, then spent the entire day avoiding me. I'm sure it wasn't hard to do. I spent the morning sitting in the principal's office at a primary school desk with my huge body smooshed into a space the size of carry-on luggage. Then I spent the afternoon in the school psychologist's office, where we talked about forming goals and developing plans. Based on his advice I've come up with the following attainable actions:

1. Forget about band entirely.

This falls under the category of Being Realistic and Accepting Reality for What It Is. No more flights of fantasy and twisted, surreal escapist imaginings.

2. Take down everything Curt put on my walls.

This will, obviously, help me accomplish step number one. It falls under the category of Removing Stumbling Blocks. Must give self every chance for success.

3. Eat many donuts.

This falls under the category of Sheer Gluttony Designed to Provide Instant Short-Term Satisfaction.

4. Sleep until dinner.

See note for step number three.

5. Shoot self.

In the immortal wisdom of *Psychology Today,* no plan is complete if it doesn't include "giving back." Do something altruistic and you'll feel 100 percent better about your life.

There it is. FAT KID WITH A PLAN. Nothing like it.

Except it doesn't work.

I arrive home and complete step number three, but that's when my plan gets derailed. I walk into my bedroom and find Dad on the floor setting up a drum set. I can tell immediately this is going to make step number one very difficult.

"Dad?" I say.

My father tightens one pedal before standing up and wiping his hands on his pants.

"Here it is," he says, as if I've been expecting this. My jaw goes slack.

"Dad?" I say again.

He comes as close to smiling as I've seen in nine years. The corners of his mouth keep moving up before he presses them back down. He claps me on the shoulder.

"No practicing after ten P.M. or before seven A.M. And I want you to learn how to take care of this set. These things aren't cheap. I want it polished, tuned, and kept in good order."

My stomach churns and I can taste the donuts rising. There's a moment of silence before I manage to croak, "I thought you didn't want me to play the drums." This seems like a problem, but my father just looks at me as if I'm missing the obvious.

"Yes," he says slowly. "But maybe I was wrong. . . ."

33.

I NEED TO FIND CURT.

I've been looking all week but he's nowhere to be found. I've been to every subway station and diner, been to The Dump twice. Everyone seems to *know* Curt, but no one knows how to *find* Curt. I'm in a panic. Dad wants me to practice, so I keep playing the stuff I used to play in junior high. I practice the things Ollie taught me. I even put on a few CDs and try to play along, but I suck. Plus, I'm confused.

Curt wants me to play because he wants a band. But maybe he doesn't want me to play anymore because I told him I wouldn't. Dayle doesn't want me to play because I'm mortally embarrassing, and Dad *does* want me to play because . . . well, I don't know why Dad wants me to play. He just does. It's my new diet.

I don't want to play because I suck.

But I want to find Curt so I can *pretend* to want to play.

And I can't find Curt.

34.

JUST WHEN I'VE GIVEN MYSELF over to despair, Curt finds me.

It's Saturday night and I'm in my room contemplating the horrible state of my life. I'm sitting at the drum set in my gym socks and Miami Beach T-shirt and I've got the sticks gripped tightly in my fleshy white fists. Only I'm not playing. I'm staring. I'm trying to decide how to tell Dad he needs to take the set back.

That's when the phone rings. I don't even consider answering it because all phone calls are for Dayle, so when my father opens my door I'm caught off guard.

"Troy, you have a phone call."

I stare, uncomprehending.

"You have a phone call," he says again. He practically wraps my fingers around the cordless phone and I hold the receiver to my ear as if I've never used a phone before. I'm like one of those little kids who doesn't know if a voice will really come out of the receiver.

"Troy? Are you there? Fuck . . . I think . . . hold on, guys." There's a lot of noise in the background and I can't tell if Curt is talking to me, or someone else. I know I should say something, but it seems impossible.

"Hello?" I say at last. There's an audible sigh of relief.

"T, man. I heard you've been looking for me. I was, um, well, you know how it is sometimes when you're somewhere else. . . ."

I'm not sure if it's a question or a statement, so I don't know how to respond. There's a loud pause in which the background noise sounds like a tornado tearing apart a small town, then Curt continues as if I've said something. He probably thinks I have.

"Good. Good," he says. "So, listen. You've got to come to this show. Smack Metal Puppets at The Dump. We're going to swing by and get you."

I look at my father, who's standing in the doorway, arms crossed.

"A show?" I say. "When is it? I mean what night?"

There's a pause, then confusion.

"What do you mean what night? Tonight. Now. It's now. We're coming to get you."

"It's now?" I repeat. "You're coming to get me?"

"That's what I said, isn't it?"

"For a show?"

"Yeah, yeah, yeah, yeah . . . Bring some cash. Okay, man? Okay?"

I'm staring at my father, thinking about what Curt has just said, wondering what this means. I'm too stunned to say no. I don't even ask him for more details. All I do is nod into the phone. It doesn't matter because Curt's saying something to someone else while at the same time trying to say something to me and it comes out as gibberish:

"So, whatsa, hey, don't, okay, be read—fuck that ma—*shiii*, okay, okay, didn't I say—yeah, good, T, bye."

The phone clicks and I'm left holding the receiver, wondering if lightning can strike the same guy twice.

35.

"WHAT THE HELL WERE YOU THINKING?"

My father's growled question is not rhetorical. He expects an answer. An answer I can't give. He hasn't lost his composure yet, but I can see the color rising on the back of his neck. He paces as he speaks.

"You agreed to go to a concert with Curt at ten o'clock on a Saturday night? You don't know what time you'll be home and you're not sure who you're going with? I'm standing right here and you didn't ask me?"

I nod stupidly.

"You agreed to do this because . . . ?"

He's waiting for me to fill in the blank but I only turn the thoughts over in my brain. *Curt called. He doesn't hate me. He asked me to a show. I have been asked to a show. On a Saturday night someone asked me to a show.*

"There's no way you're going. Call Curt back and tell him you're not going." I look at my father. I'm about to say that I don't have Curt's number when a single thought replaces all the others. *What the hell* was *I thinking? Maybe* FAT KID GETS PUMMELED BY MOB. *Maybe that.*

My father is waiting for his answer. I swallow hard.

"You're right," I say. "I can't go. No way. I can't go."

He can see the panic in my eyes. He stops pacing and shifts his weight from one leg to the other, the only sign that he's agitated.

"What do you mean you can't go?" he asks, as if he hasn't been telling me the same thing ever since I hung up.

I shake my head. "No way. I can't. You said no. You're saying no, right?"

I'm almost begging him. I've suddenly realized with perfect clarity that there is no way I can go to a show with Curt MacCrae. I do not go to punk rock shows. I do not go out on Saturday nights to hang with large crowds of people. My mind begins to swirl out of control imagining all the embarrassing things I might do. I start to envision every inadvertently funny move I'd make. Would Curt be picking me up in a car? What if I can't fit inside? Or have to cram myself in like a wadded-up ball of chewing gum? What if we get inside the building and it's too crowded and people get angry because I'm in the way? They won't be able to see. I'll slam into everyone. I'll sweat and make stupid noises and be too tired to stand all night. There'll be no place to sit down, so I'll collapse and everyone will think Curt is a loser for bringing me. I'll be dressed all wrong in my stupid bland pants and everyone else will look cool, punk, retro . . . *something.*

My father sits across from me on the bed. He's shaking my shoulders, saying, "Troy, Troy. Get a hold of yourself."

I can't force enough air into my lungs.

"What was I thinking?" I breathe at last. It comes out as a choked whisper and my father leans back and sighs. It's a resigned sigh, as if he's thinking about everything he had to do in the military and how easy it was compared to raising me. If I weren't so wrapped up in myself I'd feel sorry for him.

"Troy," he says at last. "Troy . . ." There's something in his voice that makes me look at him. My father the security expert with his crew cut and bodybuilder arms. My father with the lines etched into his face. He looks old.

"Troy, you can go to a concert," he says, whispering. "You can do this. You know Curt. You're a smart kid. If there's a problem you'll call me."

I shake my head.

"No, Dad. You don't understand. You can't understand. What if . . . ?" My voice chokes and I have to stop. I refuse to cry in front of my father. Refuse.

Dad shakes his head. He refuses to allow me to cry in front of him. "Get up," he says. "Get dressed."

"Dad . . . I . . ."

"I'll call you when your friends arrive."

My father walks out and I think, *Friends? Not friends. Friend. Maybe.* Suddenly, I'm not so sure about Curt. This could be a huge setup after all. The mother of all practical jokes orchestrated for the benefit of the entire school. Like the time someone stole my clothes after gym. It was right before the school assembly and I had to hide in the locker room the entire period listening to the roar on the bleachers outside, praying no one would come in. What if this is the same thing, only worse?

I can't get dressed. I sit on the floor in my T-shirt, sweatpants, and socks and can't move. My muscles have atrophied.

Dayle walks by twice, then stops and stands in my doorway, studying my walls. He keeps looking at the mural Curt made out of the food wrappers. It's the first time he's let on that he noticed and I wish I could enjoy this small crumb of attention. But I can't. The mural is a distant blur out of the corner of one panicked eye.

Dayle shifts his weight from one leg to the other. "Dad says you're going to a show at The Dump." He doesn't exactly sound impressed, but he doesn't sound scornful either. "Brandon's heard of The Dump. Heard of your friend, too. He says it's pretty intense there."

He throws this out like an offering, but I can't breathe.

"You're really going to go?" he asks when I don't respond.

God, I want to say yes. I want to nod with confidence, but I shake my head no. Dayle makes that noise he makes when he thinks I'm not worthy of actual words. The one where he breathes out through his nose like a horse.

Damn it, I think. *I'm bigger than you. I'm older than you. You could show a little . . .*

But I can't speak and Dayle turns around and walks out.

36.

I HEAR THE BUZZER RING TWICE, but I just sit there.

In the living room the door to our apartment is opening and I hear the sound of muffled voices. Only my father's voice is clear and distinct. He's giving orders to whoever just arrived.

"You, go in. You two. Stay where you are."

I almost laugh because it's kind of funny, the idea of Dad treating Curt and his friends like new recruits, but I'm too busy worrying about what Curt will say when I tell him I'm not going to the show. I can hear his footsteps coming down the hall, shuffling randomly as if he's not picking up his feet.

My bedroom door opens and a single bedraggled sneaker steps inside. The sneaker pauses, then allows the rest of the body to follow. Once inside, Curt looks around as if he's never been here before. He nods at the drum set, then at me. He looks tired, but otherwise the same. I was expecting some classic punk getup but he looks like he always looks, just dirtier. He's got on the same ripped jeans and my dad's Marines T-shirt. The T-shirt looks like crap now and I'm surprised Dad didn't make him take it off—out of respect.

Neither of us says a word.

"So, are you ready?" Curt asks at last.

"Nooo," I say very slowly.

"Nothing to wear?" he asks.

I pause. "Mmm. Something like that." Curt scratches his chest, then scrunches his nose, thinks, sticks his hands deep in his pockets.

"I can see the problem," he admits as if he's just completed a complex mathematical formula. He approaches my closet. My T-shirts are hung in a neatly pressed line and Curt looks at all of them twice.

He opens my dresser drawer and starts digging through my underwear.

"Wha . . . ?" I start, but Curt finds what he's looking for.

"Put this on."

He's pulled out one of my plain white undershirts, and I take it from him, wadding it up in my sweating palms.

"Curt, I don't think I can—"

"Shut up," Curt says. "The guys are waiting."

I pull on the undershirt as Curt grabs my scissors off the desk. He looks at my pajama pants—huge black sweats—and without asking cuts them off at the calf. I don't say a word, but some of my terror falls away with the material.

Curt takes out my huge marker and starts writing something on the back of my undershirt. I'm dying to know what it is—terrified that it reads DORK.

When he's done Curt pushes me toward the mirror.

"Check it out," he says. I turn until I can see the reflection of my back. He's drawn a giant letter T in 3-D block with the stem of the T making a knife. It's quick, but it's good.

"All right then," he says. There's another long pause. "So, you're still in the band, right?" he asks, as if this is totally related to my outfit. I study my reflection in the mirror.

"Yeah," I say. "Yeah. I mean, I never really . . . well, I was just hungry, see. . . ."

Curt grins and bounces once. He tries to turn the bounce into a casual stance, one arm propped on top of my dresser, but it doesn't quite work. His arm pushes my lamp off the edge and he has to scramble to pick it up. He grabs it quickly, then sets it down again, relieved.

"I thought so," he says, glancing at the door. He grins again. "Well, then," he adds. "This is an important event in the history of Rage/Tectonic, so let's go. We haven't got all night."

37.

I FOLLOW CURT INTO the living room and we both stop short because my father has Curt's friends backed against the front door. I recognize both of them, and the idea that my father is now interrogating two members of Smack Metal Puppets is almost more than I can take. Curt doesn't seem to mind. His eyes are huge and he inches forward until he's standing right beside my father, just behind his left elbow. His head moves back and forth as he watches every move Dad makes.

Curt's friends are spilling their guts.

"It's on St. Marks right near the Orco Hotel. I don't remember the cross street. I swear, I don't remember or I'd tell you. But it's on St. Marks. I know that much. I'm sure it's on St. Marks. . . ."

Dad is writing everything down on a pad of paper. Piper, the guy who's providing the information, looks like a punk version of Curt. He's small and wiry with a semihomeless look to him, but his hair's dyed black and he's got three huge tattoos. He's wearing studded bracelets with a Buzzcocks T-shirt. The other guy, Leon, is tall, skinny, and awkward-looking with no hair and huge features, like a distorted giant ostrich. Both of them could not look more relieved to see Curt, but Curt is no help. He stands next to my dad, grinning like a geek.

Dad notices him, pauses, then glances at me. If he has an opinion about my new look he doesn't reveal it. Dayle doesn't reveal his opinion either. He's sitting in the living room trying to look like he's not watching us. But his eyes betray him. They shift back and forth between me, Curt, and Curt's friends. I almost think Dayle looks nervous, as if he's hoping Curt won't notice him, but he doesn't need to worry. Curt can't stop watching Dad.

Dad takes a step back and lets his gaze linger on each one of us.

"If I hear . . . ," he starts, then stops and scratches his chin.

"If you do anything . . ." He points his finger accusingly at Curt's friends, then puts it away. Finally, he turns to Curt.

"No drugs," he says. He leans in menacingly until his face is very close to Curt's. "No drugs. No drinking. I'm holding you responsible, son. Do you understand that?"

It's meant to be a threat, but Curt swells with bliss. He looks the way I looked when Curt first called me T. My father waits for a response, then finally gives up and turns to me instead.

"Troy," he says solemnly, "have a good time at the concert."

38.

THE MOMENT THE DOOR SHUTS, I panic.

I wait for someone to say, "Who the hell is this loser?" but no one does. Leon makes a clumsy leap to touch the ceiling of the hallway and Piper makes a face.

"Did you see that? Piper was toast, man, toast!"

"Shut the fuck up. I was not."

Leon laughs too loud. "He had you squealing, man. Squealing like a pig."

This starts a fight between the two of them that Curt watches with something resembling pride. The fight lasts all the way down in the elevator and spills out onto the street, escalating as it progresses. They move from accusations of cracking under pressure to some past grievance I can't decipher. By the time we reach the car Leon has Piper in a chokehold and he's getting ready to smash his head into a dilapidated Buick.

"Guys, meet Big T," Curt says suddenly. It's an awkward moment for introductions but the two untangle themselves and Piper attempts to smooth his hair while Leon runs his fingers over his bald scalp. They're both out of breath and look like they couldn't care less about meeting me. We exchange awkward hellos, and I take a deep breath thinking, *As the Fat Kid prepares to take his final walk to the gallows, he takes a last deep breath to sustain himself through the coming ordeal. . . .*

We climb into the Buick and I just barely fit. Curt sits in the back with me, and his friends take over the front. They continue bickering as if we're not there. I stare out the window wondering what it will be like when we arrive, thinking about what Curt said back at my house. *This is an important event in the history of Rage/Tectonic.*

I glance over at Curt but he's asleep, pressed against the car door with half his face smooshed against the window. One of his sneakers has fallen off and his T-shirt is balled up in one fist. It's hard to imagine this as an important event in the history of anything.

Come to think of it, I'd settle for absolute obscurity with no humiliation.

39.

BY THE TIME WE PULL UP in front of The Dump I'm feeling mildly ill. It's a Saturday night and the Village is wired. It's a late night festival of sirens and neon, a meeting place of hip skinny people. Curt wakes up, rubs his eyes, and seems pleased with his circumstances. He nods at each of us as if to say, *Well then, here we are.* I only wish I felt the same. It doesn't seem possible that I exist in such a frenetic city.

Piper attempts to parallel park in the only available spot half a block away, and I press my face against the window. From what I can see, The Dump doesn't look at all like the place I had my drum lesson. I kept hoping it would be the same empty, dusty shack and we'd arrive to find only Ollie inside. Instead, the place is hopping. The line snakes around the corner of St. Marks and there are already three bouncers lingering outside. The blue neon beer lights are lit up and the color spills onto the sidewalk.

Curt climbs out of the car, but I stay put.

"Come on," he says, running his fingers through his hair. It's sticking up weird where he slept on it, but he doesn't seem to care. "Let's go. Let's go."

"Are you sure about this?" I ask.

Curt surveys the crowd. He appears to give my question serious thought. At last, he nods. "Yeah," he says. "Most very sure."

I force myself out of the car like a death-row inmate forces himself out of his cell to make that final trip to the electric chair. The street is packed full of purple-haired people with safety-pinned lips. No-haired people with black leather jackets. Black-haired people with dog collars. I am most definitely out of place. The closeted fan that should've stayed in the closet. I want to go home, but it's too late now.

Piper hands me his car keys. "You're the Party Master, T," he says as if he's known me his whole life. Leon nods in agreement.

I have no idea what a Party Master does, but having a title makes me feel slightly better about the prospects of entering the building. At least I'll have an official purpose. Something to justify my presence. I pocket the keys and try to decide how I'll push my way through the crowd. The walk to the door is interminable. FAT KID WALKING.

Curt pulls a bottle of Jack Daniel's from under his T-shirt and takes a long swig before passing it to the rest of us. When it gets to me I take only a tiny sip, then stifle a gasp. My skin is about to corrode like one of those dead bodies in *The Mummy.* Curt laughs and I start to bristle, but it's a light laugh, so I swallow and pretend to laugh, too. It occurs to me that, Dad or no Dad, this isn't such a bad idea.

I reach for the bottle to take a longer sip and Curt lets me keep it.

"This doesn't make you an alcoholic," he says as if he can read my mind. "And I know your father said I was to be responsible, *eh-hem,* but I think, in this case, 'responsible' could be fairly interpreted, in an executive-decision sort of way, to mean *in your best interest,* in which case J.D., which would normally qualify as 'drinking,' would simply be *a little something you need.*"

I take another sip. *Amen to that,* I think. Then I remind myself to breathe.

40.

WE WALK PAST EVERYONE who's been standing on line for God knows how long and I can feel their eyes boring into me as we pass. I will myself to become small and compact, but it doesn't work. I am huge and obese. The bouncer nods at Curt and lets us in with no cover fee. He gives me a look as we enter, but doesn't ask for an ID.

Inside, The Dump is transformed. There have got to be a hundred people packed together, pressed against the stage, and the music is playing so loud I can feel the bass in my stomach. The place reeks of smoke and a sweet smell that saturates the walls. I'm grateful for the warm distraction of the Jack Daniel's in my stomach.

I follow Curt until the crowd gets too thick, then pause wondering what to do. Curt turns around and waves me forward. "This way," he yells. I hesitate, then push my way through the crowd.

There's only twenty feet between the bar and the door, but it's slow going. Curt yells something else and I realize he wants me to be his linebacker. He squishes to one side so I can pass, and once I'm in front people get out of our way. I almost stop, stunned at this occurrence, but force my feet to keep moving. I glance back at Curt and he's cheering.

This time I do stop. *What?* I think. FAT KID SAVES THE DAY? *You've got to be kidding. . . .* I stop when we reach the stage door. It isn't really a door. It's actually a large swinging structure made of plywood with the words FUCK OFF spray-painted in red across the front. I'm sure this means me, so I don't go any farther, but Curt jumps ahead and pushes it open. Piper and Leon follow, plowing over me. Piper grabs the empty bottle of Jack Daniel's and smashes it on the floor. Every face looks up.

"The band has arrived!" Piper yells. There's a lot of hollering, smashing fists, burping. . . . Everything happens at once and my eyes don't know where to look. They keep moving to Curt, getting distracted, then drifting back again.

There's something different about him here and I can't decide what it is. He seems . . . calm. He nods at people as he passes and moves around like he's at home. Everywhere he goes he becomes the hub. Conversations shift. People touch him without his seeming to notice. The guy on the floor looks up from tuning his guitar. The girls who have been draped over the ratty couches file away without being asked. It's as if everyone knows the real talent has just walked in. The Curt I know, the one who's always trying to get something or keep something, suddenly becomes the kid listening to Beatles records. It's like watching layers of grime wash down a clean, white drain.

Could I wash away like that? If I found the right place, the right thing, the right moment, could my layers of fat wash away like grime?

Curt plants himself on the arm of the red plaid couch in the center of the room and nods at me, solemn-like.

"Everybody," he says. "There's my new drummer."

There's a moment of relative quiet while everyone looks around the room as if there's someone else Curt must be referring to. I look up, startled, and huff, waiting for the riotous laughter. It doesn't come. Ollie nods at me from across the room where he's applying spray paint to his Mohawk in front of an old, cracked mirror. Piper and Leon smash fists.

"Awesome," someone says. "Can he play?"

I hold my breath.

"Nope," Curt answers. "Can't play a thing."

There's absolute silence as everyone processes this information. Finally, a small guy in the armchair nearest Curt laughs. He's got green hair and a tattoo of a dollar sign with a slash through it. I recognize him immediately. Mike Harrington, lead singer.

"You're kidding, right?" Mike asks, glancing at me.

Curt shakes his head, grins like a maniac, and coughs twice. Mike sits up.

"Curt, that's insane," he says. "Even for you. You can't pick a drummer who can't play the drums." I can tell he wants to say more, but he doesn't. He glances at me apologetically, but I just shrug. *Someone had to say it.*

Curt takes a battered joint out of his sneaker and lights it very carefully. He takes a long hit, then passes it over.

"Why not?" he asks at last, breathing out a column of smoke. "What's the most difficult part of finding a drummer?"

No one answers, so Curt does.

"Finding someone, some *person,* who isn't a pretentious fuck and can hit hard." He grins at me. "Troy's it."

Mike laughs like he doesn't believe him. "Except for the minor detail of actually *playing* the drums," he says. "When are you going to play your first gig, 3004?"

Curt takes the joint back. "Chill," he growls.

The two of them stare at each other and for a long time neither one speaks. The rest of us shift nervously and I feel like I should be saying something to defend myself, but can't decide who I want to win the argument. Finally, Mike takes a long drag and shakes his head.

"Fucking psychotic control freak."

Curt grins. He sits down on the floor, picks up the guitar lying next to him, and starts playing quietly. He now has everyone's attention.

"Never fear," he says. "T is going to be the biggest . . . *eh-hem* . . . thing to hit The Dump since Smack Metal Puppets. Trust me on this one. He's got mass appeal."

In all my life I've never heard it put quite that way.

41.

FAT KID PROVERB #52: Never miss an opportunity to dissect a compliment.

Unpretentious. *Hmmm.* That would be a good thing, right? That would imply that I was something other than *just* a massive freak. That would imply something positive about my character. Something positive in a lacking sense, of course, but positive nonetheless. Unpretentious. A person lacking pretense. That's good, right?

I cannot wrap my mind around this new development. Despite all appearances to the contrary, Curt might actually have reasons for wanting me in his band that don't relate to food and shelter. I drum my fingers nervously.

The room has quieted down and half the people who were filling it have left to find their spots out front. Curt's warming up in one corner and Piper's trying to color in his tattoo with a girl's fuchsia lipstick. Ollie finishes spraying his Mohawk and moves over to where I sit. He looks tentative, as if he's waiting for me to explode into a million scraps of fat.

"Hey," he says.

I nod. "Hey."

"So, everything's back on track, eh?"

I flush, but Ollie doesn't seem to be making fun of me. He glances around the room. "Ever been to a show?" he asks. I cringe because I was hoping no one would ask. I consider lying, but figure I've done enough of that already.

"Uh . . . no."

Ollie whistles low.

"Never been to a show either?" He shakes his head and glances at Curt. "Well, then," he says, "prepare to be blown away."

I think he means it metaphorically, but the next minute the room literally begins to vibrate. I feel the energy drift in from outside and it feels like a tornado just before it touches down.

A small woman with dreadlocks pokes her head in.

"Five," she says.

The energy in the room shifts. Piper and Leon strap on their guitars. Ollie makes a fist and yells. The crowd outside starts screaming obscenities and I think there's going to be a riot. Mike ducks out the back door, the girls come back inside, and Curt disappears, all in a matter of minutes.

I'd get up and go out front, but I need an invitation. It's as if the moment Curt left the room I ceased to be invited. The band jokes and tunes the guitars, oblivious to my predicament, and for the first time I wish I were really with them. I tell myself to join the crowd, but my butt becomes a two-ton weight no human power can lift. I'm anchored to my chair. I can't move until someone says the magic words.

Finally, Ollie turns to me and grins. He polishes his skull ring and adjusts his piercings.

"Better find your way down front, stage right," he says. "This is going to be a kick-ass show."

With those magic words the bewitched whale, who is really a punk rock drummer cursed by the wicked sorcerer of Hostess, triumphantly lifts his butt from the chair. He battles his way across the room, and at last makes it to the door. He flings it open and . . .

I take a deep breath. I'm standing at the top of the small flight of stairs that lead backstage, a full two feet above the swarming crowd. The club is sweltering and immediately I start to sweat. My back becomes Niagara Falls and I can feel my underarms radiating. I'm descending into a pit of body heat and volume. The noise is intense; voices mixed with grating static from the amps, shifting bodies, and sirens outside. I look back as the FUCK OFF plywood door swings shut above me. There's no turning back now.

When I finally stop I'm two feet from the stage, lost in a horde of awkward freaks. There's a guy with kinky orange hair standing beside me. He's screaming, "Come on, motherfuckers," over and over again even though there's no one on stage yet. I can't tell if he's high, but his eyes are huge and shining.

Someone rubs against me and I puff. The guy to my right spills his beer and it splashes onto my leg. We look up at the same time, eyes wide, and he mouths something over the noise. I nod even though I don't know what he said, but I get the distinct impression that he's afraid of me. I stand up, confused. PUNK REBEL AFRAID OF

HYPERVENTILATING FAT KID. Now that's funny. I'd laugh if I weren't scared shitless.

I glance around the room, searching for the exit. I've never been so claustrophobic in my life. *Get me out of here,* I think. *Get me out. Get me out.* The energy is too much. I'm about to turn and push my way out when the stage lights go off and sound pulses out of the amps. The room goes pitch-black and it's so loud I can scream at the top of my lungs and not hear myself. That's exactly what everyone is doing. The mass becomes one, yelling with one voice, beckoning the band on stage. They lift their fists in the air, pressing forward like a tidal wave, and I'm caught in the swell, crashing forward, about to drown.

42.

THE FIRST SOUNDS ARE THE DRUMS. They break like thunder, unexpected, and the backbeat is set, manic and wild. I feel the smack of the drumsticks in the pit of my stomach as they snap against the skin. The crowd begins to pulse. The lights come up red as fire and the stage is hell. I look at it and sweat. The sweat drips down my cheeks, into my mouth. It stings my eyes.

I squint upward at the black silhouettes glaring down at me. I stare at them, trying to connect them in my brain to anyone I know. But I can't. They aren't those people anymore. They aren't even human. *Ollie?* I think. *Piper?* The sound is so loud I can't hear myself think. The drums go on forever, torturing us with the prelude. They toy with the crowd, saying "fuck you" before the music's even started.

Then the lights go up and Mike leers over us. He doesn't say anything, just starts singing. Screaming really. His voice is a wailing falsetto, and he lets the sounds grate like a challenge. The guitars take up the call. Piper's on bass and Leon's the lead and they dip in with the refrain, pushing their lines until Mike's ready to add words to the milieu. All my attention is up front and I'm straining forward waiting for the words to come.

Mike opens his mouth and Piper leaps into the air as if he's been shot, almost falls backward, but pulls upright at the last moment. He doesn't care. He thrashes like a small demon while Leon strides across the stage to loom over him. They make two opposite, unnatural curves. Mike finally releases the verse, letting it crash over the audience.

Born in the U.S.A., ain't got fucking much to say, don't we all want it that way?

It's the most amazing thing I've ever seen in my entire life. The band raises the challenge and the mass of bodies gives its answer through the smashing of fists, faces, arms, and legs. People are hitting me from all sides, careening into me, then crashing off again, but I just stand there. It hurts, but in a good way. The kind of way that makes you pissed at the world. Makes you think you could turn around and smash them back. I start to move, ever so slightly, then harder, wilder.

The movement answers the song. I'm watching Mike's face as he sings and he's really asking the question. *Ain't got fucking much to say, don't we all want it that way?*

I pound my fist into the air and holler until I think someone can hear me.

43.

I AM A PARTICIPANT.

With one gesture I've moved from the world of imagination to the world of funky sweat stench and ear-ringing volume. The guitars screech, the sound shakes the club, and the best part is, no one's looking at me. I'm six-foot-one, three hundred pounds, and *no one is looking at me.* I'm one of the many. In fact, I'm more than that. I'm one of the few. I'm the one who knows the band.

I thrash forward, staking my ground, letting the body heat soak into my skin. For once I enjoy sweating. I lap it up. My sweat is the salt water left over from the tidal wave. I'm short of breath from yelling so loud. Each song builds on the first, never letting the energy subside. The second song is about sex and I feel my head ready to explode. A woman in black leather winks at me across the room and suddenly I'm a fucking sex god. My body swells until I fill the room. I'm not fat. I'm enormous. I look out over the crowd and think for the first time, *I could be bigger.* I could be even bigger. . . .

I imagine this is what it would feel like to try the best drug ever invented. My head's spinning, my guts are pounding, my body is soaked. I'm thinking, *It doesn't get any better than this. Nothing is better than this.*

Until they introduce Curt.

He comes on after the first break. It's been over an hour of relentless, in-your-face songs and the audience is fatigued. People stand breathless during the break, arms limp, eyes glazed. The crowd mills aimlessly, semistoned, and I wonder how the Puppets will bring them back to life.

What I don't realize is, they won't. Curt will.

When the lights go off again there's a swell of anticipation. I'm exhausted, but the people beside me are watching, waiting. They know what's coming. . . .

Mike climbs back on stage and grabs the microphone in both hands. He holds it close to his mouth, breathes heavily, staring at us, knowing what we want.

"You all know what's next," he growls. The crowd roars.

"You all *know* what's next," he repeats. He smashes the microphone onto the floor and the sound system screeches. He yells in his true, raw voice.

"Curt MacCrae."

The lights go black and the sound of Curt's guitar wails over the audience. He plays a chord that sounds like the scream of someone being murdered, then the lights are back, blazing red, and Curt is center stage. I'm fully expecting his arrival, expecting what I heard at the subway, or at his house, but when the sound hits, my arms fall slack.

Curt isn't Curt anymore. He moves with energy, plays with abandon. He's everywhere and nowhere. He plays like he's pissed at the world, but grins the whole time. Makes me feel like a starving man given a burger, then prime rib. The band joins in, but Curt plays circles around them. He's two steps ahead, pushing, augmenting, twisting the music into something else.

There's something almost frightening about it. He doesn't look up between songs, and he throws his body around—crashes to the ground when he sings, *"Frustration is my only friend,"* leaps into the air at the first hint of manic lyrics, lies to us, pleads with us, tells us the truth. He smashes into the drum set, plays on the floor, cuts himself on the microphone stand, and bleeds all over the stage. The crowd can't take their eyes off him.

His guitar progressions make me itch because they're too fast, too loud, too constant. My brain can't keep up. His voice is deep and raw. It's the exact opposite of everything he's playing, cool to the guitar's hot. First he's angry, ranting into the microphone, then just when you're surging with adrenaline his voice cracks and he lets you see what's behind the anger.

The crowd responds. The energy's the same, but the mood moves from manic to primed. The surges become deep, forward grooves rather than short, spastic thrashing and the fists linger a second longer before they pull back. Chaos turns to intent and by his third song Curt could lead us anywhere. *Anywhere.*

And the thing is, he doesn't want to. He doesn't give a fuck. He's into his music and nothing else. There's no agenda. No moral to the story. No call to arms. Curt's the same skinny, blond guy without a wardrobe, but he's singing his guts out about life. *Life.* Smack Metal Puppets sing about rage, but Curt sings about the look on a rich man's face when he hands you money. The Puppets sing about fear, but Curt sings about waking up nowhere, when it's dark out and you've got no fucking clue where you are. And the whole time he's singing the guitar is saying everything Curt won't. It's so clear I almost hear it in English.

I can't describe what it does to me. I'm moving, then I'm still, but all the while I'm thinking, *That's me. That's me up there. That's my life he's singing about.*

I glance around the club and notice that no one is drinking. No one yells to their friends or sees me looking. They're all watching Curt and I imagine every one of them wants to be his best friend. He's the vortex of the whirlwind.

People start climbing on stage and the bouncers try to push their way up front, but it's too late. First one, then two, three, four people climb up. They have their moment in the spotlight, then dive off again. It's as if Curt's saying "This is *your* show" and they're taking it back. We've passed from the question to the challenge and everyone knows it.

The trickle turns into a stream and people are leaping from the amplifiers. I catch them without even thinking. Cheer them on. Part of me wants to rush up there, too, to leap into the void. . . . Maybe this time I'd take flight.

That's when I truly realize what I've stumbled into. It's the first time I see what everyone else sees when they see Curt MacCrae. He *is* a legend. And he's picked me to be his drummer.

44.

THE SHOW'S OVER WHEN CURT leaves the stage. The crowd screams bloody murder for an encore, but Curt won't come back. He's gone. *No dessert.* The band keeps going, but the thrashing is lighter, and people start to leave. The Puppets smash all their instruments to compensate.

I stand with the crowd until the club lights come on and people start to disperse. I stare at the spot where Curt stood. Some guy comes up to me and screams in my face. He's so drunk he can barely move, but he can yell "Motherfucking concert" until he's hoarse.

I turn away and let myself think what I've been wanting to think all night.

I came here with Curt MacCrae.

The crowd thins and I pry my way to the stage door. There's a couple passed out on the floor beside the stairs, a guy with a bleeding lip hanging on the railing. Five women are planted on the steps, combat boots blocking my way.

"Hey, soldier," one of the girls says. She's looking at me, clearly expecting a response, and I wonder what spectacularly embarrassing thing will come out of my mouth.

"Coming through," I say at last. My voice doesn't crack and I look up, shocked. I sounded almost cool. Casual, even. I start to grin and my chest heaves.

The girl nearest me giggles. She's wearing a tight black skirt and a shirt that spills off her shoulders. I stare at the exposed flesh like it's going to leap out of her shirt and attack me.

"Didn't you come in with Curt?" one of the girls says.

I nod stupidly. *Yes,* I think. *Yes, yes, yesss.* She drapes herself over my arm and smiles drunkenly.

"Then I'm with you."

The rest of the girls laugh.

"You're such a whore," one of them says, but two more of them attach themselves to me. Their skin is actually touching my skin. On purpose. Voluntarily. I cease to breathe. My lips pucker and I choke on my own spit.

"Well, come on," says the girl in black. "Let's go find Curt."

I tell myself I *must* enjoy the feeling of three girls hanging on me. I must because it may never, ever, ever happen again. *Goddamn it, I must. . . .*

But I can't. Later, I'll probably jerk off to the mere recollection, but at the present time it's too much pressure. I have to walk without waddling while pushing my way through a crowd. Breathe without huffing while trying to suck in my cheeks. To make matters worse, one of the girls keeps bumping into things and I can't tell if it's because she's drunk or because I'm steering her wrong.

"Sorry. Sorry 'bout that. Sorry." Every two seconds I'm apologizing.

I pray Curt's nearby. I scan the crowd, looking for his blond hair and ratty shirt, but don't see him. The girls are looking, too. I can tell. They're hanging on me, but their eyes never stop scanning the room.

Everywhere, there are people talking at once and I catch

snatches of conversation. Stuff about the show and how soon until the next gig. Every now and then I catch someone talking about Curt. I'll see a head bobbing and hear someone's voice say, "Where'd he go, anyway?"

I'm running out of places to look when I hear a voice yelling right by my ear.

"Still have my car keys?"

It's not a voice I recognize. One of the girls disengages from my arm and squeals while I turn almost full circle to see Piper. He's standing on his tiptoes with the girl now planted firmly beside him. She beams and Piper ignores her. He's totally smashed.

"What?" I yell. "Where's Curt?"

He sways precariously and gives me the thumbs-up sign. "Yeah!" he says. "Yeaaahhh!"

I watch as he disappears with girl number one, and realize that soon there'll be no girls at all. I keep making the rounds until finally I find Ollie dismantling the drums. He's drenched in sweat and rivulets of red paint leave blood marks down his face.

"Where's Curt?" I yell. Ollie looks up. He's on his knees adjusting a foot pedal. The second girl disengages and repositions herself near him. She gets in his way and laughs for no reason. Ollie looks at me, then looks at the girl and shakes his head.

"Curt's gone, man. Sorry."

I stare at him, uncomprehending. I turn and stare at the last girl, knowing I've just lost my one and only shot at getting laid while still in high school. She detaches from my arm.

"What do you mean?" I say, desperately. I want to shake him. Dislodge the right answer. "He can't be gone. I came with him."

Ollie just laughs.

"T," he says, "no one comes with Curt. He always comes with you."

45.

IT'S LATE. THE CROWD'S GONE HOME, and
I'm sitting outside in the cool night air, drenched in sweat, T-shirt
clinging to my chest. The girls have disappeared and The Dump is
shutting down, but I don't care. I have no idea how I'm getting home
and since I'm still holding Piper's car keys I have no idea how he's getting home. I have no idea where Curt's gone. It's 3:45 A.M. My ears
are ringing. But none of that matters.

I'm grinning like a massive lunatic.

Who would've thought? I muse. *Who would've imagined I had it in
me to be such a stud?* Never mind that I'm sitting out here alone with
no way to get home. Never mind that the girls were looking for Curt.

This is the best night of my entire life.

"Still here?"

A voice startles me from my reverie and I look up. It's Ollie. He's
standing next to me, hands in the pockets of his leather jacket.

"Need a lift home?" he asks. I shrug as if to imply I'm not desperate, then get up as quickly as my body will allow, afraid he might
leave without me. Ollie laughs.

"Still got Piper's keys?" he asks. I pull them out of my pocket and
jangle them. Ollie nods.

"That's good because Piper left with that girl, so we're driving his
car home. Mike and Curt went to some party and . . . hey," he says,
"what happened to your entourage?"

I have the distinct feeling he's making fun of me, but it doesn't
matter. Ollie can laugh all he wants and I won't even drive myself
crazy about it. *Yet.*

I hand over the keys feeling as if I've just completed an important
mission, and this time, when we climb into the Buick, I sit in the front.

Ollie pulls out and I turn all the way around to watch The Dump fading away behind us. When I can't see it anymore I turn around and start talking. I don't mean to, but once I start I can't shut up.

"That was the best thing. I mean, damn, when Curt was up there playing and the crowd started climbing on stage . . . I caught this one guy who dove off the amplifier and I swear he would've splattered if I hadn't been there. He was careening to the floor and I wasn't even looking and then, *bam,* he's crashing into me. I was like one huge fucking air bag. Oh, man . . ."

I keep moving back and forth and just can't stop. We're heading down Houston Street and the lights outside are blurry and freaky and everything I think seems *very* important. Finally, Ollie cocks an eyebrow in my direction.

"You're high," he comments at last. It's a general observation, but it strikes me as pure genius. *Yes. That is definitely it. I am completely high.* Then the panic hits. If Dad finds out . . .

"Holy shit." The thought is sobering.

Ollie laughs. "You're not *that* high," he says, his voice cracking on "that." "You just breathed in a lot of that *sweeet* night air. . . ."

I turn the thought over in my brain, wondering if Dad makes a distinction between "high" and "*that* high."

"Think it's okay?" I ask at last. I'm worrying about Dad, but I'm also wondering about Curt and Mike. I'm wondering what kind of party they went to and why Ollie didn't go. Maybe he hates drugs and thinks I'm a loser. I wait for the hammer to fall, but Ollie just shrugs.

"Yeah," he says, glancing at me. "I think it's okay if you don't get caught up in the bullshit. You don't seem like the kind of guy who'd get caught up in that."

I stop moving and look suspiciously at Ollie. *Was that a compliment?*

It occurs to me that I might *want* to be the kind of guy who gets caught up in the bullshit. I'd sell my high-school soul to get caught up in the bullshit if it meant I'd be cool for a day. I don't say that to Ollie, though.

"You seem like a good guy," he's saying. "I think you'll make a decent drummer for Curt. He needs someone to be a strong beat under the guitar line, know what I mean? He needs someone solid. Someone who'll tow the steady line, freak out when he needs you to freak out, and rein in when he's on the ledge. Lots of people can't do that. They've got to turn him into something he's not. But you . . . I think you might be the one."

It's the coolest thing anyone's ever said to me and I have absolutely no idea how to respond.

"Next street over," I say. Ollie makes the turn and follows my extended finger to double-park beside my apartment building. I mean to get out of the car, but don't. I have to make sure I got it right.

"So, what you're saying," I ask at last, "is that you think I'd make a good drummer for Curt?"

Ollie shrugs. "Yeah," he says. "I guess that's what I'm saying."

I slide out of the car.

"Ollie?" I say. He squints at me, twisting his skull ring.

"Yeah?"

"I think I might."

46.

I, TROY BILLINGS, FAT KID extraordinaire, could make a good drummer for Curt MacCrae. The words have been uttered and there is no taking them back.

I lie on top of my covers turning the thought over in my mind,

drumming my fingers incessantly. Drum, drum, *drumdrumdrum* . . .
I try to shut my eyes, but next thing I know, they're open again, staring at the ceiling. I turn onto my stomach, but that doesn't help. I
stare at the dark silhouette of my drum set, my brain on turbo.

Drumdrum . . . drumdrum . . . I think about the concert, remembering every vivid detail. Hot air inside the club, crowded bodies, a
girl's ass rubbing against my thigh, violent thrashing, something un-
contained. I picture myself on stage, playing the drums behind Curt.
I don't look so bad. I mean, I don't look *funny.* I'm almost sure of it.
Or maybe I do and no one's looking. They're all watching Curt.

Drumdrumdrum . . . I think about being part of the crowd. The
music swirled like smoke and I was breathing it in like everyone else.
This may not seem like much, but when you're fat, people get annoyed
when you breathe. It's their space. Their world. And usually they're
right. Usually the world belongs to skinny people. But not tonight.

Drumdrumdrumdrum . . . I think about me. I imagine myself on
stage, a huge shape that's *meant* to be huge. The crowd spreads out
below me, pounding their fists into the air and waiting for me to
bring my sticks crashing down. All those hands reaching for me. All
those eyes looking at me. I wonder if they'd laugh. Maybe they
would. Or maybe they'd scream louder than they'd ever screamed before. Without even trying I'd be king of the freaks.

47.

THE NEXT MORNING I WAKE UP drowning in cot-
ton. The first thing I notice is the smell of cigarette smoke from last
night's clothes. The second thing I notice is the coating on my
tongue. Putrid.

"Damn." I roll out of bed and glance at the clock. It's almost noon and I'm starving. The sun shining through my window is annoying. And did I mention I'm starving?

I shuffle to the kitchen hoping Dad won't be around. He's not, but Dayle is sitting at the kitchen table eating corn flakes from a pie pan. He's used all but the last inch of milk. *Bastard* . . .

I don't say anything, but Dayle does. Right away.

"Dad went out," he says as soon as I walk in. I glance at him but don't respond. Seems to me I didn't ask.

Dayle waits a beat. "Yeah, he went to the store. Said not to wake you because you didn't get in until late. I should've anyway because you were snoring like a hog."

I scowl, but don't take the bait. I'm taking a lesson from Curt, making my little brother work for my attention. Dayle keeps eating, but he looks over at me every now and then.

I take out a chicken potpie and stick it in the microwave.

"What time did you get home, anyway?" Dayle asks.

I rub my eyes for effect.

"About four-fifteen."

Dayle's eyes bug out and he momentarily forgets to play it cool.

"Dad didn't freak out?" he asks. I give him the look.

"I'm a senior, you know. He wasn't even awake. At least, he wasn't in the living room. . . . Besides, you can't go to a club and leave early. The show didn't start until midnight." I pause, then casually add, "You should've seen Curt. He was incredible. He played at the end of the set and people were climbing on stage, diving off. . . ."

The timer rings and I take the potpie out of the microwave. Dayle watches me slide it onto a plate.

"You're such a liar," he says. "There's no way you went to that club. No way."

He says it the same way he always does. *Pompous.*

But this time he doesn't look so sure.

48.

THE PHONE RINGS EARLY Monday morning. Too early. Dad's getting ready for work and Dayle's hogging the bathroom. No one calls at 6:45 on a Monday morning.

"Hello?" My voice betrays skepticism.

"Yeah, hello?"

"Yeah?"

"Hello?"

I'm stuck in a twilight zone conversation that can't seem to begin.

"Who is this?"

There's a pause.

"It's Curt." The voice sounds unsure. There's a lot of noise in the background and I swear I hear an announcer saying, "Chicago. Last call for Chicago."

I cringe. "Where are you calling from?"

I have visions of Curt halfway across the country calling to tell me it's over. No band. The phone crackles and he coughs into the receiver.

"You want to meet today?" he asks. "We could meet at your place because mine's mostly off-limits for . . . indefinitely."

My heart stops pounding and I let out a long breath.

"Okay," I say, slowly. Then, afraid I'll miss out on the opportunity, I say it again more enthusiastically. "Yeah. Okay."

Curt sounds relieved.

"Cool," he says. "I'll come over and we can practice the songs I played at the club. I set up another lesson with Ollie, but not until later in the week. That's okay, though, because we gotta work on timing and—" Curt's on a roll but I'm watching Dad walk past my bedroom door.

"Wait," I say. I have to say it twice before Curt listens. "Wait. I can't skip class anymore. I got in trouble last time. We can practice here, but it's got to be after school."

There's a long pause. So long I can hear the entire announcement asking everyone to check their personal belongings.

"You won't skip?" he says at last.

"I can't," I say, then hurry to cover my ass. "But I still want to practice. The concert was incredible. You were *awesome. . . .*"

I can almost hear Curt nodding, stuffing his hands in his pockets.

"But you won't skip?" he asks again.

I pause, wondering if I should recant. Every Fat Kid cell in my body is screaming for me to do it, but a voice is whispering in my ear, saying, *Don't risk it, don't risk it.* I glance at the empty hallway.

"No," I say finally. "Sorry, but it's gotta wait until four forty-five."

49.

WHEN I GET HOME it's 4:20 and Curt's waiting. Actually, he's sleeping in the hallway outside my apartment, his guitar leaning against the wall behind him. I have to nudge him with my foot to wake him up. I don't ask how he got through the security door. I'm not sure I want to know.

For his part, Curt looks surprised to see me. He's squinting and his hair's all matted to one side.

"Troy. Yeah. Right. I just got here." Curt's barely awake and already he's distorting reality. There's something funny about that, so I chuckle.

I want to say, *How stupid do you think I am?* But I don't. I just open the door with my key and let us in. I keep looking over my shoulder at him and he gets annoyed.

"What?!" he says.

I shake my head.

"Nothing. Nothing. It's just . . . you seem . . . different."

Curt makes a weird face. "Well, I didn't take anything if that's what you think . . . ," he says, but that's not it. I'm looking for the Curt that was on stage. The one who was so honest it was painful. The one who seemed like a rock star. Now that we're at my house, sitting in my room, I have a hard time believing it was really him. *Who was that masked man?*

Today, he's hyper and erratic and can't get through a whole song without stopping. He's supposed to be teaching me the music but he leaves out big chunks and refuses to sing any lyrics. He starts out playing one thing, then merges into a totally different song without warning.

It's not going well and it gets worse when Dad gets home. Dad issues an executive order that Curt will be staying for dinner, and this is good because it makes Curt happy, but it's bad because now Curt can't pay attention long enough to play *anything*. He keeps running into the hall to check on the progress of dinner.

Dad's a good cook when he wants to be and the apartment fills with the smell of roast beef and gravy and Curt's practically sweating by the time it's ready, then all of a sudden he doesn't want to go. He lingers in my room and says he thinks we should practice the intro one more time. I look at him like he's insane, partly because I know he's hungry and partly because when Dad cooks, promptness is required.

I have to work hard to herd him toward the kitchen, and when we finally get there the table's set and Dad and Dayle are already sitting down. *Welcome to the Cleavers.* Until Curt and I join them.

I sit next to the roast beef and mashed potatoes and Dad passes the peas and bread. As usual Dayle hogs the quart of milk. We wait for Curt to sit down, but he stands in the doorway looking nervous before sliding in next to Dayle. He folds his hands as if he's about to pray, looks up, notices we're not praying, and unfolds them guiltily. Dad glances at the clock to indicate that we've lingered too long, but he doesn't say anything. Just passes the bread to Curt.

There's a lot of shuffling as the food gets passed and I sit back to watch the drama. It's twisted of me, I know, but I kind of enjoy the intense discomfort of it all. Everyone looks pained and for once I'm not the cause. Tonight, I am the most comfortable person in the room. I watch them all like a sociologist.

First, there's Curt. I know Curt's uncomfortable because he's restrained. He doesn't show any excitement except in the corners of his eyes, and he's very careful to sit still. His napkin falls off his lap repeatedly and every time it does he glares at it as if it's betrayed him. When he bends down to pick it up he tries not to bend his body, as if that might count as too much movement. Soon he's engaged in an all-out secret battle with the napkin that culminates in a covert stabbing with his fork.

Then there's Dad. I know Dad's uncomfortable because he doesn't speak. He limits himself to nods of encouragement or censure and keeps his posture perfect. This means he has to stifle his desire to correct Curt's posture, which is not perfect. Consequently, his grip on his knife tightens until his fingers turn completely white.

And of course, there's Dayle. I know Dayle's uncomfortable because . . . well, I wouldn't have known it if I hadn't seen him dish the roast beef, but as soon as he lifts the serving fork I know. He takes one portion instead of five even though he's desperate to gain weight, and he never once looks at Curt as he passes the tray.

Curt, however, takes five helpings, then puts half of it back. Then he retakes half of the half he just put back.

Dad takes a deep breath as the scene repeats itself with the mashed potatoes. And the peas. And the bread. Finally, Dad can't stand it any longer. He sets down his knife and turns to Curt.

"So," he says. "Do you have a job?"

It's the last question anyone was expecting and I cough like I'm hacking up a lung. Curt chokes on a pea and I wait for it to come flying out his nose, but he manages. He drinks his entire glass of milk to recover.

"Ummm . . . Yes. Occasionally," he says at last. He screws up his face as if he's thinking really hard, then coughs into his napkin. "I get paid to play guitar sometimes," he says in a muffled way.

This is not the correct answer and Dayle squirms in his chair. I have an intense desire to make hand signals under the table to feed Curt the correct responses.

My father eats a forkful of potatoes very intently.

"I meant," he clarifies after a pause, "do you have steady employment?"

Curt sinks into his chair, becoming one with the wood. He takes a miniscule bite of bread and I can almost see him shrinking. He looks around the kitchen, stares at the refrigerator, taps the left tong of his fork.

"*Well,*" he says, drawing the syllable out. "The answer to that would be, most technically . . . no."

Dad looks smug. At least as smug as Dad ever allows himself to look.

"Have you *ever* had a job?" he asks, leaning back in his chair. He eats more steadily now, systematically finishing one food before beginning the next. His attention is perfectly divided between Curt and the mashed potatoes.

Curt on the other hand stops eating altogether. He nods enthusiastically. "Yeah. I mean, *yes,*" he says carefully, "plenty of them." Then his smile fades midthought. "But I tend to get fired."

Dad's just about to take a bite, but he looks up, his eyebrows shooting high on his forehead. I can tell he wasn't expecting the tag line.

"Why do you get fired?" he asks as Dayle and I exchange glances across the table. I wince, Dayle looks frantic, and Curt frowns, shrugs, then finally sighs loudly.

"Well," he says. "I steal stuff and sleep when I'm not supposed to."

Dayle sputters. He knocks over his glass and milk sloshes across the table. He wipes it quick with his napkin, apologizing profusely. My eyes bug out and Dad's fork makes a jagged path through his peas, raking them into the gravy.

"Why would you do that?" Dad asks, completely off guard. His brow is crinkled and his cheeks actually puff just a tiny bit.

Curt looks around the table. He pauses, then sets his jaw. He takes several bites of food at once, just in case it gets taken away, and with his mouth full he says, "I do it because I'm hungry and I'm tired." He swallows hard and takes several more bites very quickly. He eats intently, but never stops looking at Dad.

I lean back in my chair and let my jaw drop to the floor. To my knowledge, it's the most defiant thing anyone's ever said to my father. It's at least the most defiant thing anyone my age has ever said to him.

Dayle and I stare, wide-eyed, waiting for the drill sergeant to take over, but Dad leans back and sets down his fork. He nods slowly.

"I see," he says at last, and passes Curt the roast beef.

50.

DAYLE IS SO IMPRESSED it's not even funny. He pretends not to be. He stands by the sink rinsing the dishes and complains to Dad.

"It's Troy's night to do the dishes. I did them last night and the night before. . . ."

He keeps stealing glances at Curt, who's trying to help clear the table but is really just getting in the way. Curt takes each plate and hands it to me to hand to Dayle. He almost drops two of them, but Dad ignores the near catastrophes and grabs a beer out of the fridge. It snaps with a hiss.

"Troy will do the dishes this weekend," he says. He looks at me with something *almost* resembling pride. "Right now the guys have to practice."

I stand in the middle of the kitchen holding a gravy-covered plate in one hand. It drips over the side onto the floor with a splat and I lean down and spend a long time cleaning it up. Long enough to grin like crazy before standing back up.

Skinny people, eat your heart out.

FAT KID'S BACK IN THE GAME.

51.

SITTING IN MY ROOM after dinner, I tap away at the drums while Curt picks out a simple melody and sings under his breath. It sounds good, and I try to tell him, but he won't hear it.

"I should go," he says. I look up.

"What? Dad said you could stay over."

He shuffles his feet, unplugs his guitar, and runs his fingers through his hair.

"I don't know." The statement lingers before he finishes it. "I mean, when would he want me to leave? Because this practicing has to be long-term. For the band. Sometimes it takes a long time to get gigs and we've got to see it through, see?"

I don't see, but I nod anyway. I'm prepared for skepticism about my commitment. Not only did I already threaten to quit, but when you're fat, people naturally assume you aren't committed. They think you're not disciplined because if you *were* disciplined you wouldn't let yourself get fat. A + B = C.

So I'm prepared with my defense.

"I totally understand," I say, oozing confidence. "I want you to know that I am one hundred percent committed to learning the drums. I've thought about it a lot since the show, and I know I can do it."

I take a deep breath. "I'm sure it seemed like I was going to wimp out on you after the first lesson with Ollie, and *I was,* but that's just because I hadn't been to a show yet. I didn't know what it could be like. But now that I have been . . ." My cheeks turn red and I huff. "Now that I've seen what it's like I know that's what I want. I never felt, you know . . . part of things before. It was as if I . . . well, what I'm trying to say is that if you and Ollie think I can be a good drummer, I'll work my ass off. Starting now. That's a promise."

I've just delivered the Fat Kid equivalent of the Gettysburg Address. I hold my breath waiting for Curt to laugh. A fat kid being overly sincere. That's got to be hilarious, *right?* But Curt only frowns and looks embarrassed.

He waits a long time, then says, "Okay, but when does that mean I have to *leave*?"

52.

I'M A SWEATING FAT KID practicing the drums. I come home from school and my day's been shit, but do I turn on the television? No! Do I hang out in the kitchen eating Little Debbie Snack Cakes? No! I go straight to my room without passing Go and without collecting two hundred dollars. The drums become my Little Debbie Snack Cakes.

I practice with or without Curt. Sometimes he shows up and sometimes he doesn't, but I'm there, regular as a high-fiber diet, sitting on the throne. I even buy myself a book. *Drumming for Dummies.* Dummies seems too kind, almost like a compliment, but I buy it anyway. I read it cover to cover, then buy four more books and a video. I go home and practice rimshots and overtones. I practice playing with different feels, in different times. I play along to every CD I own.

All the while I'm thinking, *This is not funny and anyone who says it is can go to hell.* I'm working my ass off, just like I said I would. Dayle comes home from practice and I'm playing. Dad comes home from work and I'm still playing. The neighbors scream, but I *still* keep playing. I play until my arms hurt and I'm out of breath, huffing away like a stranded porpoise. I'm a total freak, but that's no one's problem but mine. Mine, damn it. Mine with a capital "M."

I am the Rocky Balboa of obese drummers.

53.

IT'S BEEN TWO WEEKS and Curt's listening to me practice. He hasn't said a word in over an hour and it's not 'cause he's asleep. He's lying on my bed with his feet propped against the wall, watching intently. I've screwed up twice that I know of, but there's been no response. I'm starting to think he's stoned, but then he gets up and takes out his guitar. He plugs it in and starts a wicked intro that blows me away. He looks back at me over his shoulder.

"Keep up," he says.

It's not a song I've heard and I'm positive I'll screw it up. And I do. I fumble the sticks and come in a fraction of a beat behind Curt no matter how hard I try not to. Then I notice he's changing the rhythm. He waits until I'm committed then cuts out, waits a beat, and comes back in with a new guitar line. I think, *Is he messing with me?*

He is, but not in a bad way. He tries to suppress a devious grin and keeps glancing over his shoulder to see if I've caught on. I pretend I'm clueless, but the next time he starts a line I launch into a loud drum solo instead. It's clumsy and ends with a huge crash of the cymbals, but it's good enough.

"Fat Kid's Revenge," I say.

I don't mean to, but I say it just as Curt's about to launch into his guitar line and it throws him off. He messes up, then his eyebrows shoot to the top of his forehead, and his face splits into a huge grin. He wrinkles his nose and starts a high-pitched screech, which he follows with a cool riff.

"Skinny People Fleeing in Terror . . . ," he says midway through. This cracks him up, and it cracks me up that it cracks him up, so now we're both laughing. I have to work hard at coming up with something new on the drums. I end up using the bass drum pedal over and over again, like the footsteps of approaching doom.

"Jocks Everywhere Run For Cover." This amuses Curt to no end.

"Perfect People Piss Their Pants. . . ."

"Rich Bastards Abandon Bank Accounts."

I drill the snare and Curt plays something vaguely related. We sound like crap, but we're playing loud and hard and it feels good. I push the tempo as fast as I can until even Curt can't keep up. He's thrilled. He lets the guitar land on one screaming note, then smashes it against the floor in exultation. I think he might throw himself into the drum set, but at the last minute he changes his mind and falls onto the floor instead. He lies there catching his breath.

I almost join him, but then I get a better idea. There's only one thing that could follow such an awesome jam session. One thing left to complete the night. I wait for Curt to look up.

"Dinner?" I ask.

The look on his face is worth all the money in the world. I've just created Curt Heaven and we both know it. His eyes light up and for a moment he doesn't say a thing. Finally, he speaks directly to the ceiling.

"I knew it," he says, solemnly. " *'Curt,'* I said to myself, *'this is the coolest person you will ever meet.'* "

It's the moment in my life I've been waiting for ever since I gained weight. The camera zooms in, the music swells, the crowd does the wave. I want to laugh or cry, or laugh *and* cry, but in the end I only sit there and blink, knowing the moment will disappear as soon as I take my next breath.

54.

I CAN'T WAIT TO HANG OUT with Curt again. Saturday I have my second lesson with Ollie and Curt's supposed to meet me there. I'm looking forward to it, but it's raining and the subways are crowded, so I arrive frustrated.

The only time Ollie can meet is early in the morning, so I'm barely awake when I get there. I've gotten up and dressed in my stupid tan pants with a T-shirt I hate that reads BIG DAVE'S GRILL. I tried to think of something creative to do with the outfit, the way Curt would have, but my brain doesn't work that way. I see bland tan pants and think bland tan pants. Big Dave's Grill is Big Dave's Grill. I wish I'd tried harder because my pants make my ass look enormous. I have the Empire State Building of asses. Some people have a bad hair day—I have a bad ass day. I'm positive Curt will take one look at me and change his mind about my being the coolest person he's ever met.

I stand under the overhang outside The Dump waiting for Curt to show up, but he doesn't, so I finally go in. I make my way to the spot where I stood during the show. Ollie's on stage setting up the drum set.

"Hey," I say. He looks up, laughing at something, and nods at me. I swallow hard and try to think of something to say.

"I'm psyched for our lesson. I've been practicing." As soon as the words come out of my mouth I roll my eyes and think, *Moron.* That sounded stupid. Ollie doesn't seem to think so, though. He grins and ambles to the edge of the stage. He's wearing a studded collar and black leather pants that shine like Vaseline.

"Good," he says. "Curt says you're sounding pretty decent already."

I look around hoping Curt arrived before me, but Ollie shakes his head.

"Nah. He's not here. He's headed to Mike's for the semiannual Be Kind to Curt Fest."

I must look confused, because Ollie snorts. "Mike's parents are born-again Christians who feel obligated to be charitable to the only homeless person they know. Every six months or so, they invite Curt to live with them. It's supposed to be 'long-term' but it lasts about three days before they kick him out." Ollie shakes his head and spits. "It's always a huge scene, too. Curt steals half the medications from their medicine cabinet; Mike chooses that weekend to pierce his tongue. Trust me. It's a blast."

He runs his hand over his Mohawk. "Don't know why they bother. Mike wants to piss off his parents, of course. Expose them as hypocrites. But I don't know why Curt does it. . . ."

He waits as if he expects me to say something, maybe contribute to the conversation, and I *want* to. I do. I mean, I'm thinking about what he's said, it's just I don't know what to add. It never occurred to me that Curt wouldn't be here. That he might go *live* with someone.

Ollie waits, then frowns.

"Well, come on," he says at last. "Might as well get started."

He lets me get settled at the drums then demonstrates a few techniques in the air and asks me to try them. I'm trying to pay close attention, but now I can't help thinking about the fact that Curt's not here. For the first time, it occurs to me that I know nothing about Curt. He's my best friend, *my only friend,* but I don't know where he actually lives or what he does when he's not with me. Today I do, because Ollie told me, but usually I just wait for him to show up. Or not show up.

I wonder why he never told me about going to Mike's. I move to hit the drum and my stick slips from my hand and crashes to the floor. The hairs on the back of my neck rise and I turn lipstick red.

"Sorry," I say.

Ollie doesn't seem to mind. He hands me my stick and starts to correct my technique. He's demonstrating the way I should've done it, telling me to hit the rim as the heads of the drumsticks hit the drum, but I'm not really watching. After a minute he starts aping around, twisting his sticks under his leg like a basketball player making an exaggerated slam dunk.

"That," he says, "is what you should've done." He's waiting for me to laugh, but I'm preoccupied.

"Hey, Ollie," I say at last, "when's Curt coming back?"

55.

CURT COMES BACK MONDAY AFTERNOON, but he's grumpy. He wants me to *keep up* and I can't. He wants me to stop *hesitating* and I don't. He plays his original stuff and it's incredible. He's never let me listen to it in practice before, so I'm distracted. I lean forward to listen when I should be adding my part.

Curt mumbles the lyrics as if he doesn't want me to hear them. I pick up only a few words. Lonely. Vomit. Cheese. A phrase—*work full-time just to make them treat me decent.* He distorts the choruses so they're just screaming and I can't tell what he's going to do next, so by the time he does it I've missed it. I come in too late. I don't hit the drums hard enough. He *hates* me.

Curt flops down on my bed.

"Life is shit," he says.

I want to ask him what happened at Mike's, but I can tell he doesn't want me to. Every time I start to speak he changes the non-existent subject.

"So, this weekend when I had my lesson with Ollie—"

"Did I ever tell you about the group that smashes entire pies on stage? I think they suck."

I nod in agreement. "You told me twice," I say. "Just two minutes ago. Anyway, what I was going to say was—"

Curt kicks at my dresser with his Converse sneaker.

"It's not exactly *fair*. Don't you think? I mean, if you had extra pies lying around you would share them, wouldn't you, T? You would never hoard them, or throw them away, say, when someone else was standing right there hoping to eat some pie. You just wouldn't do that, would you?"

I shake my head. "No, but—"

Curt's face turns red. "I say screw people who hoard pie. Who needs to listen to goddamn gimmicky bastards from the suburbs who don't know shit? They shouldn't be allowed on stage, and, furthermore, maybe someone *should* steal from them. That's what I think. . . ."

The thoughts are rapid, random, and unfiltered. He kicks harder and harder at my dresser until my lamp crashes to the floor. I pick it up, desperate to find some way to enter the conversation, but by the time I open my mouth, Curt's packing to leave.

"Fuck that," he says, slinging his guitar over his shoulder. "I don't need to stick around *anyplace* I don't want to." He kicks my wall hard, then glares at it, then at me, then points accusingly.

"Like I said, life is shit."

"Curt," I say, "couldn't you just stay for din—"

He rounds the bend and disappears down the hallway without another word. I follow him to the apartment door, but by the time I lug my huge body down the hall he's gone. I curse myself for being too slow, for ever thinking of hoarding pie, for not coming up with the right thing to say. *Maybe life is shit,* I think.

All I want is for Curt to come back.

56.

IT'S WEDNESDAY AND CURT'S BACK. On the one hand I'm glad, but on the other hand he's *really* grumpy. Almost angry. Almost angry *at me.* I thought I was cool. The one person who would share my pie. But apparently I'm not. I'm sure it's because I still suck at the drums and he's determined I'll never make it as a drummer. When I ask, he says, "Yeah, that's what it is." But I wonder because he still wants to practice.

The rehearsal is miserable, but I invite him to stay for grilled cheese anyway. He hardly talks the whole time, and when we're standing in the kitchen he stares out the window as if I'm not there. It's raining and water is collecting on the sill. Curt's fixated on it. He keeps running his fingers through his hair.

"You got any painkillers?" he finally asks.

We do, but I say no. Curt kicks at the table leg.

"Cough medicine?"

I shake my head, and Curt gets grumpier.

"Fuck that," he spits. "Doesn't anyone ever get sick around here?" He rakes his fingers over his face as if he might gouge his eyeballs out and I just stand there awkwardly, listening to the butter sizzle in the frying pan.

"I don't want grilled cheese," Curt says at last.

This is a surprise and I'm annoyed because they're already made.

"What?!"

I don't think it's unreasonable for me to question his decision, but Curt shoves his chair backward and it falls with a crash.

"I don't *want it*," he says, harshly. "I'm going . . . *somewhere*."

He storms out of the kitchen and I stare after him, wondering where he'll go. I think he's left, but later I find him asleep in my bed with every blanket on top of him. I have to dig out an old afghan and sleep on the couch. When I wake up in the morning he's gone.

57.

IT STOPS RAINING ON THURSDAY and Curt shows up at my locker unannounced. I can tell right away that things are better even though he looks like crap. He stands next to me and drapes his arm around my neck—no easy feat—and manages to look semicasual while talking to his small crowd of admirers.

"So we'll be playing at The Dump, T and me, and we're going to, *eh-hem*, do something *new*, so if you're there you will see this new thing in its newness."

The kids look impressed. The bell rings and Curt says, "I'd tell you more but me and T gotta do lunch. Strictly a band thing, you know?"

Curt follows me to the lunchroom, then hangs around while I go through the line with my tray. I keep glancing over my shoulder to see if he'll disappear, but he doesn't. He's busy turning away people who want to sit with us. With him, I mean. For the first time in four years I actually have someone to eat with and it's an amazing feeling. Truly amazing. I find myself staring at all my classmates, thinking, *So, this is what it feels like to be them.*

I'm so enamored of Curt's presence that I give him almost everything off my tray. My small tub of applesauce, my green beans, one of my three sloppy joes, even my dessert. He grins and licks the chocolate pudding bowl with his tongue.

"Sorry I was grumpy," he says with his head tipped back and the bowl poised over his face. The apology comes and goes rather quickly and I'm almost not sure I heard it. I try to think of the last time someone apologized to me, but can't recall the occasion.

"It's okay," I say, then clear my throat. A guy can't go getting all teary-eyed in the school cafeteria. "No big deal," I huff. We sit in silence while the noise around us rises to a crescendo.

"So," I finally ask to break the spell, "what's this new thing we're going to do?"

Curt looks blank, and I have to remind him of the speech he made at my locker just moments ago. His brows knit. He itches his nose, then drums his fingers on the table.

"I said that?" he asks. I nod in the affirmative and he sighs.

"Guess we'll have to think of something."

58.

THERE IS NO NEW THING. There is only the same thing, which gets old very quickly. Practice. Practice, practice, and more practice. As the days progress, I have to mentally detach from everything I ever imagined about being in a band.

Fat Kid Dreams of Being in a Band:

When I imagined myself in a band, it was always fun. The word "band" conjured up hot chicks screaming for my jiggling body, fabulous music played at top volume in huge arenas, and adoring fans throwing themselves off skyscraper amplifiers. I pictured myself in tailor-made 2XX leather pants and a black beret, dark glasses pulled down as I ooze out of the limo.

Reality:

Curt and I in my bedroom trying to scrub half a bottle of NyQuil out of my carpet before Dad gets home. I've got gas and Curt's pissed because his guitar string broke, he lost his pick, and I won't lend him ten dollars because I've already loaned him twenty this week. It's only 8:30, but Dayle's trying to "power sleep" in order to improve his football game, so every time we actually start to play something he throws his cleats against the wall. My fingers have blisters and my fat gets in the way when I try to play anything fast.

We've got two weeks before our first gig.

"Better double our practice time," Curt says.

59.

FAT KID DIES OF EXHAUSTION.

I am caught in a warped PlayStation 2 game in which the object is to drive your obese drummer insane by using one or all of the following weapons available to you: lack of sleep, excessive motion, infrequent meals, constant nagging, or the Mother of All Weapons— the ray gun of mind-numbing terror.

The gig is this weekend and it is quite possible I may not survive to see it. We've not only doubled, but tripled our practice time, and

Curt is working me intensely on three songs—all ones he's written. I can't add anything to them, but I can *almost* do what he tells me. I can do everything *except* hit the drums hard enough. That's our sticking point.

It's Monday night and we're on our fifth consecutive hour of practice with only a miniscule break for dinner. I am expiring while Curt stands in the center of my room with his arms crossed. For the fifth time today he's seriously pissed.

"What the hell are you doing?" he yells.

"I was doing exactly what you told me to do," I say, which elicits a snort of derision.

"Fuck that," he answers. "You're like some chick that's afraid to make too much noise. You're an anorexic chick letting her nail polish dry. You're a goddamn anorexic cheerleader."

I huff and my cheeks balloon.

"All right! I get the point, but I'm telling you I'm hitting as hard as I can. What do you want from me? The neighbors keep complaining and my father's in the other—"

Curt cuts me off.

"Shit. Don't blame this on your dad. He's getting into our music. I can tell. He wouldn't be letting me in here if he didn't get off on it. You're just acting like a pussy."

Now he's making me mad, so I toss my drumsticks on the floor. This pisses Curt off even more.

"See?" he says. "See? What the hell was that? If you were really mad you'd throw them against the wall. Shove them up my butt. Stick 'em up your nose. But *no*. You've got to toss them onto the carpet. What the fuck is that?!"

The color is rising in my cheeks but I don't say anything. I'm thinking about rage. Huge tectonic plates grinding. Curt narrows his eyes. He walks slowly over to my drumsticks, picks one up, and very deliberately breaks it over his knee. His eyes are locked on mine the whole time and I want to punch him, but I don't.

"Fine," I say. "Fuck you. Now see how we'll fucking practice." I cross my arms over my chest and for a long time neither of us says anything. Then Curt looks at me and shakes his head. He lets out an exasperated sigh.

"Go get some duct tape," he says at last.

60.

THE CLOSER IT GETS to the gig, the more I'm convinced I've made a mistake. *Another* Fat Kid–sized mistake.

It's two days before the gig and I still can't play the drums. Oh, I can play better than I could before. Five lessons with Ollie and marathon practice sessions have accomplished that much, but I'm still no punk rock drummer. All my illusions of concave grandeur are proving to be just that . . . illusions.

I stand in front of my mirror and stare at my reflection. My crew cut is still a crew cut even though I'm trying to grow it out. My T-shirt with the inane slogan still stretches thin across my continental stomach. My fat still drips over my waistband like an overflowing vat of lard. My face still sports sagging pockets of flesh and triple chins. My fat lips still pucker like the kid in the *Far Side* comic that's always collecting bugs.

In the past two weeks I've morphed from Rocky to roadkill. I'm repulsive and no matter how much I try to fool myself, people *will* laugh. They will hold their stomachs and piss their pants. They'll point and when I try to get off stage they'll trip me and laugh some more. They'll call me "fatty" and "lard ass" and "blubber." I'll think, *You unoriginal mental midgets with brains the size of rabbit shit,* but I won't say that. I'll wait for Curt to defend me, but in the end, he'll side with the skinny people because he's king of their world. He'll say, *Why couldn't you just keep up? For God's sake, how hard is that?!*

61.

THE DAY OF THE GIG I start to feel sick. It comes on as nausea first thing Saturday morning and soon morphs into full-scale plague-ridden disease.

I climb out of bed and feel my way blindly to the kitchen. My father is standing at the sink in his boxer shorts, sipping a cup of coffee. The smell makes my stomach turn. He glances at me, oblivious, then returns his attention to the window.

"So, Curt tells me you have your first gig tonight," he says casually. He says it the way the man in the Folgers commercial says, "Folgers is a real bargain and tastes great, too." Dad never says anything casually.

I'm reaching for the saltines, but stop with my arm extended. *Please, God, no,* I think. *Do not let my father go to the gig.*

Dayle comes in from the living room tossing a tennis ball up and down. He's dressed in his football jersey and blue jeans and looks like he's ready to win the Super Bowl while I'm ready to heave into one.

"Yeah, Curt told us about the gig," he says, joining the conversation without an invite. "He said you're going to rock. He said you're awesome, Troy. Can you believe that? Curt told me you can really play the drums and he said we should come tonight. . . ."

I can't take it anymore. I bolt from the room and lock myself in the bathroom. About a minute later I hear Dad's voice outside the door.

"Troy?"

I don't answer.

"Troy?" he says again. "Are you okay?"

The question is absurd. Am I okay? Have I been okay for the last nine years? Does it seem "okay" that I am locked in the bathroom?

"Yeah, Dad. I'm fine."

There's a long pause and I wonder if he's gone away.

"Curt said you might be a little nervous," he says at last.

I'm starting to wonder when Curt did all this talking. It occurs to me that, despite everything, it may not be worth it to have such an annoying friend. Why couldn't I have found a nice, normal friend? One who collected rocks and enjoyed perusing the *TV Guide*? Of course, if I'm honest, Curt found me, but that's beside the point. . . .

"I'm not nervous, Dad," I say. It's a total lie, yes, but how do you admit you're debilitated by fear to a man who has crawled through jungles on his stomach carrying a knife in his teeth? "I'm fine," I say again.

I hear Dad move. I hear the sound of his huge body slumping against the bathroom door and picture him in his boxer shorts and undershirt sitting on the floor, trying hard to think of anything to say to his disappointment of an eldest son. I wait for the textbook sermon on fortitude.

There's a long silence.

"Troy?" Dad says at last. "I'm proud of all the hard work you and Curt have put into this. You kids have worked diligently and that's to be commended."

I'm sitting on the toilet with my head in my hands, but I look up slowly.

"Dad?" I whisper. My voice breaks.

I move to the door and open it an inch, but he's gone. I stand there anyway, a half-dressed Fat Kid blinking back tears in an empty hallway.

62.

BY MIDAFTERNOON I'M FEELING slightly better. Curt arrives and we run through our entire set, just like we usually do, but it's like pulling teeth. I can't keep the beat and Curt seems distracted. He yawns and hops and retunes his guitar. We struggle through an hour of practice before he flops backward onto my mattress. He crosses his legs and his toes stick out of the holes in his socks. I set down my drumsticks and move over to my dresser. I dig around until I find him some decent socks, then toss them across the room.

"Your feet smell," I say. Curt grins. He puts them on and pulls them up over his pant legs halfway to his waist. It occurs to me that it's the first time I've seen him smile in weeks. Maybe it's because we're practicing all the time, but he seems thinner and dirtier and more serious than he used to.

"You think I'm ready?" I ask. I pray he says yes, but Curt's face goes all slack and dumb like it does when he wants to lie. He makes an exaggerated show of thinking.

"Well, umm, in some facets I suppose, yes, but in other ways kind of no," he says. He studies the wall. "You're technically really good. I mean, really . . . but maybe you're missing some miniscule thing. I don't know this for sure, but maybe you're not *listening* to the music." He taps his fingers rapidly and wipes his nose on my bed-spread.

I want to tell him that he makes it pretty hard to listen some-times, but I don't. I can feel the acid churning in my stomach.

"You think so?" I ask. "I mean, I'm trying to listen. . . ."

Curt shrugs, adjusts his socks, and looks away.

"Maybe you're too self-conscious sometimes." He frowns. "Maybe you're thinking about yourself instead of the song . . . possibly." He pauses and shoots a glance at me. I can tell he's trying hard to make me see something, but I just can't get it.

"Drumming's about how you relate to the music," Curt says. His face morphs from dumb to intent, the way it always does when he starts talking about music. He stares up at my ceiling. "Anyone can play a beat," he says, "but the great drummers listen to the sounds around them, then add their own part in the conversation. They *influence* it. Know what I mean? You can't think about yourself when you play, even if you're thinking bad things, because, well, that's still thinking. . . . See?"

For the first time ever I feel myself shrink. I clutch the drum-sticks until my fists turn white and Curt screws up his face until he looks like a ferret again. He shifts uncomfortably and studies the wall.

"You'll do fine tonight," he says. "Really. You'll do great, but I'm just saying that maybe you're missing the point. That's all I'm saying. I'm just suggesting you play the music, not the drums. That's all."

It's a good speech and I want to respond. I really do. But I'm busy morphing from obese guru of self-consciousness to tiny speck of worthless foam.

63.

TWO HOURS BEFORE THE GIG:

I can't stop thinking about what Curt said. He's gone on an errand, something very important that came up just after he told me I suck. We've agreed to meet at the club, and he's given me the complete lowdown on the gig. *Theoretically,* it's doable. If I weren't such a loser.

We're to play three songs as the opening act for the Stoned Rollers. We'll open with "Lonely," then move on to "Fucking a Cat" and "NyQuil." If I feel confident I'm to add something to the conversation. If I feel panicky I can fake it by simply playing a steady backbeat while Curt does the rest.

I'll be faking it. The weatherman predicts a zero percent chance of confidence today. It's hateful with a chance of suicide.

64.

ONE HOUR BEFORE THE GIG:

Dad dropped me off just moments ago, promising on my mother's grave not to show up with Dayle. I considered trying to climb in the trunk while he was pulling away, but it was locked, so now I'm sitting backstage at The Dump surrounded by people, staring at the wall. I can't think. I can't remember my name or how old I am. I can't remember how I ever allowed myself to get to this point— forced into making an ass out of myself in front of a potentially violent crowd. *How exactly did this happen?* Even for me it's mind-boggling.

People stop trying to talk to me and I concentrate solely on breathing. I hear the crowd out front and my breath becomes ragged. The Stoned Rollers aren't as popular as Smack Metal Puppets and Curt comes by repeatedly to tell me that there's no one here. It's *freaking empty,* he says. But I know better. I hear them waiting.

After a while, Curt sits beside me and smokes pot. I have a feeling he's doing it on purpose so I will accidentally inhale his smoke. He removes three unidentified pills from a prescription bottle, swallows them with beer, then drums his finger in wild time to something inside his head.

Ollie comes backstage to see if I'm okay.

"You look a little pale," he comments, but I don't respond.

A girl I don't know sits on my lap and I hardly notice. She says, "Everyone's nervous their first time" in a sexy voice, but instead of making me hot it makes me want to puke.

Curt watches me and shakes his head.

"Shit," he says. I can see the caption above his head. SKINNY KID MAKES BIG FUCKING MISTAKE.

The noise outside increases in volume and the lights dim. The dreadlocked woman sticks her head in.

"Time," she says.

My stomach churns. Curt stands up and shakes his body like a boxer getting ready for a fight. He hops in place, spins in a half circle. His eyes look glazed, and he shrugs unnecessarily.

"It's just three songs," he says. "No big deal. If we suck, we suck. That's what you've got to tell yourself. We're not doing it for them. We're just, well, you know . . . *playing music.*"

I realize I'm supposed to get that by now, but I can't even nod. Ollie stands behind Curt and surveys the scene.

"I don't know, man," he says. "He's not looking so good. . . ."

Curt shakes his head, quick and decisive. "No way. He'll be fine. He'll be great. T is the essence of punk rock, see, and once he gets out there he's going to kick some serious skinny ass." He smiles, and picks up his guitar. "Yeah," he says again, as if convincing himself. He looks over at me.

"All right," he says. "Let's get this show on the . . . uh . . . yeah. Let's go."

I stand behind a makeshift curtain waiting to be announced. *How absurd is that?* Me, waiting to be announced. Me, Troy, who has made a lifetime career of trying to disappear, am now standing behind a curtain waiting to be ANNOUNCED.

Curt leans toward me.

"Play *anything,*" he says. "Kill time until you're ready." He's starting to get nervous. To doubt his judgment of me. I stare straight ahead.

I hear someone on the other side of the curtain say our name. They say it splashy-like. *"Rage/Tectonic."* I'm in a dreamy state, contemplating the sound of the announcer's voice.

Curt slides on stage and plays the opening chord then looks back at me, still stuck halfway behind the curtain. The crowd goes wild as Curt glares at my incapacitated form. They don't know why, but they know he's pissed. He plays the entire first song while I do nothing but watch. He plays it loud and mad and it sounds good.

I watch intently, thinking I should leave, but after the song ends, he stops and says, "I've got a drummer for this one." He motions me out and I swear my limbs won't move. They're thick like Silly Putty. My nausea increases.

I waddle on stage and for the first time see the mass of faces below me. They're everywhere, looking up expectantly, and I can tell they're waiting for me to screw up. Waiting for the Fat Kid to look like a moron so they can laugh and laugh.

I take my place behind the drum set and my brain turns to helium. Everyone stares, waiting for me to pop.

Curt buys time by tuning his guitar. He looks back and talks low under his breath.

"Don't bail on me," he whispers. "I swear to the big fucking A, Troy. Don't bail on me."

I don't respond. I'm staring into the audience, knowing I cannot lift my fat arms in front of all these perfect, competent, skinny people. I can*not* pretend to be a rock star. My nauseous stomach lurches as if I've just crested the top of a mammoth roller coaster. I can taste the bile in my mouth and then . . .

I am Mount Vesuvius.

Everything I've eaten for a week erupts. Canned ravioli, leftover pizza, Ben and Jerry's ice cream, mashed potatoes, Twinkies, Sprite, pretzels, bean burritos . . . I am the mother of all volcanoes.

There is stunned silence. Absolute and total silence. There's vomit everywhere, covering the stage like Pompeii. I wait for the laughter, and decide that when it comes I will literally die. I will stop my heart by sheer force of will.

Then I hear it. Someone *is* laughing. It's Curt. He stares, wide-eyed, grinning like he's just seen the best show on earth.

"Holy shit," he says. He turns to the stunned crowd.

"How's that for punk rock?" he asks them. He grins, then says it again louder with both middle fingers extended. "How's that for fucking punk rock? Now that was a very new thing." He screeches his guitar and the crowd goes nuts.

65.

I SHOULD STAY. REALLY, I SHOULD. Curt has just saved my life. For the second time. I should stay to clean up the drum set. I should stay to apologize to Ollie.

I don't stay.

I make a stupid bow, playing along with Curt's charade, then leave the stage in a haze, waddling back the way I came. I hear the crowd yelling, cheering, thrashing, leering . . . but I don't see them. I don't see Curt either, even though I hear him playing. I'm only conscious of walking, one foot in front of the other until I'm off, through the back room and out the exit. I don't breathe until I'm outside.

I stand in the alleyway behind The Dump, right next to the Dumpster. It's overflowing and smells like shit. I puke again onto the sidewalk, then wipe my mouth with my T-shirt. A rat crawls by and I shoo it away. Nearly makes me sick again, but this time I hold it in. I keep thinking, *This is the worst day of my life.* I try to remember every horrible day just to be sure, then I confirm it. Yes, short of the day my mother died, this is the worst day. It ranks number one uncontested on the humiliation list.

I step around loose garbage to reach the curb, then hail a cab. While I wait my eyes get all red and puffy. I ignore them, concentrating instead on the putrid taste in my mouth. I look down at my shirt to see if there are any stains. Of course there are. It figures. It just figures.

I shake my head and think, *Well, at least it must've been funny.* I'm sure it was funny for someone. It was funny for Curt, right? Curt laughed right away. The audience laughed once he did.

He saved my ass, there's no denying that, but I hate that he laughed. Why did he think it was funny? It wasn't. It wasn't fucking funny.

A cab pulls up, and I rub my eyes, then turn to stare at The Dump one last time before climbing inside.

66.

I TELL DAD I'M SICK and he lets me stay home from school for three days. Curt calls fifteen times, but I ignore his calls. Ollie calls twice, but I won't talk to him either. Instead, I eat.

In seventy-two hours I eat an entire Entenmann's cherry cheese danish, one whole lasagna, five corn muffins, three cans of Chunky soup, two bags of Doritos, one can of Pringles, a package of Oreos, six bagels with cream cheese and jelly, eight fried eggs, a box of Wheat Thins, leftover turkey and stuffing, three-quarters of a meatloaf, and three cans of SpaghettiOs. I eat everything in the cupboard but refuse to leave the house to buy more. I imagine myself stepping onto the curb in front of our apartment and everyone in Manhattan doubling over in laughter, or vomiting when they see me.

I tell myself I'm doing the world a favor by staying inside.

FAT KID MARTYR.

I don't practice the drums the entire time. I sit in my room and stare at my drum set, but absolutely do not pick up the sticks. Dad asks what's wrong, but I won't tell him. Would you admit to your father that you threw up on stage at a place called The Dump? I don't think so. Dayle doesn't even ask. He assumes I've screwed up, but I don't care. He's right, so I just think, *Fuck him. That's how it's going to be. End of story.*

Except for Curt.

Or maybe I should say *except for Ollie.* It's Ollie who gets my attention.

Thursday afternoon I'm watching television when the phone rings. I've been avoiding the phone all week, but I figure at this point I'm safe. I'm reaching for the scrap paper to take a message for Dayle when I hear the voice on the other end. It's Ollie.

"Hello?"

I pause. Part of me, the same part that turns purple and starts huffing with embarrassment, wants to hang up immediately. But another part is curious, so I clutch the phone tightly.

"Hello," I say. There's a sigh of relief on the other end.

"T, is that you? I've been trying to reach you all week, man. I kept getting your kid brother and he told me he was giving you my messages but . . ."

He pauses, waiting for me to make some excuse about not getting them. I don't.

"Well, anyway," he says, "I was hoping you'd come back for a few more lessons. I could use the money."

FAT KID CHARITY. I see *right* through him.

"Thanks," I say, "but I don't think so. I'm not really cut out to be . . ." I choke on the words and Ollie jumps in before I can say anything else.

"Listen," he says, "I know you're embarrassed about the gig, but you shouldn't be. You're a fucking legend now, man. I've been trying to get through to tell you. Everyone thinks it was a stunt and a goddamn cool one at that. People ask about you. They talk about the great vomit incident." He laughs. "It's not as big a deal as you think."

I put down the bag of Doritos and turn off the television, conscious that my body is suddenly alert. I want to believe him, but I threw up all over the freaking stage. It doesn't get worse than that.

"Thanks," I say, "but I really can't."

There's a long pause. I think he's going to hang up, but he doesn't and when he talks again he almost sounds angry.

"Fine," he says, "but if you're not going to come back for you, then at least do it for Curt. He thinks you hate him because you won't return his phone calls. He knows you're home because he's been sleeping in the park beside your apartment building."

I choke. "What?" There's a clicking sound on the other end and I imagine Ollie's huge skull ring clicking against the receiver.

"Yeah, well, don't tell him I told you, but he has been. Curt has a hard time when people bail, you know. I keep telling him you're just embarrassed, maybe you need some time to get over this, but he's not doing so good. . . ." He pauses, then speaks carefully. "Now, I'm not telling you what to do, but if I were you I'd get my *ass* up and find him. I think he's moved to one of the subway stations now. . . ." He pauses again, waiting for my response.

"Ollie," I say.

"Yeah?"

"Thanks."

67.

I HAVE A GOOD IDEA which subway station Curt will be in. I make my way to Second Avenue and start scouring the place. Filth-stained underground pit that it is, I don't see how anyone could sleep here. Ever.

I look gingerly, not wanting to touch anything, and I'm being so careful that I trip over Curt before I notice he's there. Suddenly, I'm falling forward and down, belly first onto the food-stained, spit-splattered concrete. My body becomes a wave tank of flesh, rippling back and forth until I skid to a stop. My chin is bleeding and a small crowd stares in morbid fascination. INSTANT FAT KID FETISH.

Curt wakes up pissed. He sits up, frantic, then glares at me from his position on the floor.

"What the hell did you do that for?!" he asks. "Can't you tell when a person is sleeping? You don't wake a guy up like that." His brow furrows accusingly.

I'm trying to get up, but can't get my balance. I'm on my knees in a patch of gum, feeling the blood trickle down my chin. The woman nearest me opens her mouth then closes it again and again, like a fish.

"Sorry . . . sorry . . . sorry," I say to the crowd, then wonder what the hell I'm sorry for. No one else has blood trickling down their chin.

"Sorry," I say again, this time to Curt. For the first time he seems to focus.

"What are you doing down there?" he asks.

I'm halfway up, so I shrug.

Curt runs his fingers through his hair and says, "Well, it's a good thing you're here because you *so* fucking owe me dinner."

68.

WE'RE AT THE DINER and Curt is slumped against the PLEASE WAIT TO BE SEATED sign. He looks terrible. Worse than I've ever seen him, and he won't talk to me, just pops his dirty feet out of his sneakers then slides them back in again. He sneezes, closes his eyes, and makes a strange noise through his nose. Everyone looks over.

"How you been?" I ask when the silence stretches too long. "I mean . . . since the gig?" It's a stupid thing to say. Anyone with eyes can tell how Curt is. He's got dark lines permanently etched into his face, a bruise on his left temple. His hair's so dirty it looks brown.

Curt grins.

"Good," he says, quickly. "Really good. I've been writing new stuff. You know, for when we practice again. I figured you'd come back. I figured it. . . ." His voice trails off and he picks at the chipped plastic on the sign. I open my mouth to say something, but that's when our waitress comes up. It's the same waitress we had the first time and she looks sexy.

"Look who's back," she says, smiling. She takes a longer look at us and her smile fades.

"Aren't you two a pair," she comments. I think she means fat and skinny, then realize she means bleeding and filthy. She's staring at my chin, and at Curt.

"Over here," she says, nodding at our table. She puts one hand on her hip and I watch her wrists turn out. My body reacts against my will and I have to slide quickly into the booth.

Curt sneezes and wipes his nose with his sleeve. He puts his head down.

"Don't feel good," he mutters, then closes his eyes.

"Sorry," I say, but it's not what he wants to hear. His head snaps back up.

"Don't be fucking sorry," he says. "Why are you apologizing for my snot?" He picks up the menu and pretends to read it, then slides it to the front of the table and sinks down low.

"I'm fine," he says, "and if you hadn't woken me up I'd feel better now."

I nod, but I can't stop staring.

"Sorry," I say again without thinking. I cringe and Curt glares.

"Forget it," he says. "I'm not speaking to you anymore."

It sounds final, but two minutes later he asks, "How much money you got? And *then* I'm not speaking to you."

I reach into my pocket to pull out a twenty.

Nothing but lint.

I reach in again, stretching out the fabric of my tan pants as I raid my empty pockets. I know I had a twenty. I know I did.

"It must've fallen out when I tripped," I mutter.

Curt frowns, surprisingly unfazed. He reaches into his own pocket and takes out a twenty.

"Fine, be that way," he says. "Now you owe me twice. . . ."

69.

I STARE AT THE TWENTY, then back at Curt. He ignores me and changes the subject.

"Why'd you bail?" he asks, staring at the saltshaker.

The question is unprompted. I squint at Curt, and he drums his fork on the table, but won't look me in the eyes. He asks the question casual-like, as if it's just any old question, but there's an edge to it. I almost say I'm sorry, but catch myself in time.

"I don't know," I say slowly, then realize it's a lie. "No. I mean, I do know." I huff loudly.

"I can't pretend anymore," I say. "It's got nothing to do with you. I'm grateful for everything. Really. And we can still be friends . . ."

Curt puts his head down on the table. No matter what I say, he won't look up.

We sit in silence until the waitress comes over and sets down three glasses of water. I'm so miserable I almost don't notice her. Then she picks up a napkin and dips it into the extra glass. I'm expecting her to wash Curt's face with it, like a mom might do for a toddler, but she reaches over and dabs at my chin.

Curt, the diner, the twenty . . . everything vanishes and I'm so damn aroused I think I'm going to explode right there in the booth. She reaches out and actually touches my skin with her skin. It's an accident—a by-product—but it happens. FAT KID GOES TO HEAVEN.

She dabs at my bloody chin and I get the most incredible close-up of her breasts. The top button of her blouse is unbuttoned and I can see the crack leading down to her bra. My mouth opens unconsciously and I let out the loudest huff I've ever made.

"There now," the waitress says. "That's better. What do you want to order?"

Curt looks up for what I think is the first time. "Chicken soup," he says quickly. He watches me watch the waitress and there's a spark in his eyes. A spark resembling an idea.

As soon as the waitress leaves, Curt perks up. He kicks me under the table.

"You are so hot for her," he says. "Do *not* deny it."

I blush and shake my head, feeling my fat move from side to side. I wonder if the waitress felt the fat on my chin, and try to remember if her hand made an indent, or if it just brushed past. Then I catch myself and remember why we're here.

"That's not the point," I say, but Curt scoffs loudly.

"Of course it's the point. Tell me you're not sitting there with your legs crossed."

My cheeks flame and puff and I wonder if the waitress would be disgusted by me. For that matter, I wonder if all the women I think about would be disgusted by me. I'm mortified, but then I chuckle.

FAT KID GETS A HARD-ON. Could be kind of funny . . .

Curt laughs, too, then stops suddenly and looks me straight in the eyes.

"She'd fuck you if you stay in the band," he says. "I guarantee it."

I'm stunned.

After all that's happened Curt still sits across from me, giving me the sincerest of his most sincere looks and I realize that not only does he still want me to be in his band but he's actually trying to manipulate me into doing what he wants.

The thought is so stunning it requires me to swallow very hard, repeatedly. He's been pissed, pleaded ignorance, implied that I owe him for a dinner he's buying with my money, and now he's promised me that a forty-something woman will sleep with me if I'm his drummer. The last was the tip-off. The idea that anyone would ever sleep with me is so absurd I know it's a con.

I swallow again, unsure what to do. The waitress brings our food, and Curt gives her his biggest smile.

"We're in a band," he says, looking endearing. "It's an offshoot of punk, but I think you'd like it." Then, as an afterthought he adds, "What kind of music do you listen to?"

The waitress sets down a bottle of ketchup. It's for me, but she sets it beside Curt.

"Oh, I don't know," she muses, distracted by Curt's sniffling. "I like Billy Joel and Fleetwood Mac. Bonnie Raitt . . ."

Curt considers, frowns, then pushes the hair out of his face in a confident way.

"You'd like us, then. We're a punk version of Fleetwood Mac, with fewer people. We have a gig in another week." Curt sneezes hard into his soup and rubs his sleeve over his nose. "I'll be better by then," he adds, as if he hasn't just done something very gross.

The waitress's brow crinkles in sympathy.

"You'd come, right?" Curt asks. "To our gig?"

Her lips part slightly, and she tilts her head.

"Of course I'd come," she says. She pauses. "More water?"

Curt is triumphant.

"See?" he says, after she leaves. "I told you."

He's waiting for me to blush, or laugh. To huff and go along with the charade. But for once, I can't. I look at Curt with his drippy nose and tired eyes, and remember our first meeting when he lied to my dad about us having a band. *Why me?* I think. *Why the Fat Kid?* Why *still,* after the worst of all horrible things happened and I threw up, upchucked, vomited, spewed all over the stage at our first gig? Why?

Before anything else can happen, I must have the answer to this one question.

"I don't get it," I say.

Curt leans against the wall, oblivious. "What?" he asks.

"Not what, why?"

"Why what?"

I take a deep breath. "Why do you want me to be your drummer? I left. I bailed. I sucked. Everyone laughed. Why do you still want me to be your drummer?"

It's a simple, straightforward question, but Curt looks confused.

"No one laughed," he says. "Who laughed?" He rubs his eyes, but I won't let him off the hook.

"Just tell me why. Why me?"

Curt frowns, then looks serious. Almost serious. He ruins it by sniffing loudly.

"Musically," he says at last, "I absolutely need a drummer. That set would have destroyed people with a drummer behind it. And I know which drummer I want. You *are* punk rock, T. You just don't know it yet, and I don't know how to convince you."

I say nothing and Curt blows his nose into a napkin. He sneezes, waits, and after a few minutes, when I still don't say anything, he squirms.

"Aw, man," he says. "Don't make me spell it out."

I make him spell it out.

He sighs, then crinkles every saltine packet as he empties the crackers into his bowl.

"Aw, fuck," he says. Then, "All right. All right, fine, but I'm warning you: When you believe something, when it's *sacred,* you're not supposed to talk about it. It's like talking about God. People need to shut up. But, for you, because I want you to be my drummer . . . because it's the most important thing . . ."

He pulls too hard at the saltines and the packet flies open scattering crumbs over the table. Curt frowns but doesn't scoop them up.

"It's like this," he says. "People say, 'Curt,' they say, 'music is dead. There's nothing new coming down.' And that's true. Only it's not the music that's dead. Music never dies. Music is what we create it to be, right? It's something else that's dead." He stops as if he's finished. "Get it?"

I shake my head, so he tries again.

"It's like when people say, 'Curt,' they say, 'why don't you dress the part? Put a little effort into it? Invest in some fucking hair dye.' And on one level they have a point. I'm the laziest fuck in town. I never have any money. I get sick all the time. But that's my point. That's why I'm a great musician."

I stab a forkful of hash browns and try to comprehend what he's saying.

"You're a great musician because you defy conventions?"

It's the first thing I've said in a long time and Curt chokes on his soup. His eyes bug out and he looks around quickly to make sure no one else heard me.

"No! No, no, no! *God,* you got that wrong."

My cheeks turn the color of bacon. I almost say I'm sorry, but Curt rushes on. He rubs at his eyes. Moves all his silverware. Whispers.

"This is why you shouldn't talk about this stuff. You can't tell it."

I nod as if I understand, but I don't. Curt leans back in the booth.

"Let's try something else," he says.

70.

I'M SUPPOSED TO WATCH PEOPLE EAT.

I'm to watch a certain couple seated at the counter until I've figured out exactly what Curt's talking about. Why I'm the essence of punk rock. I've been watching for half an hour now and I see nothing.

"What am I looking for?" I moan. This is starting to annoy me, and I'm beginning to think Curt's avoiding the issue. He takes out his used napkin and blows his nose again.

"You'll know it when you see it," he says for the fifth time.

I roll my eyes and go back to staring at the couple. As near as I can tell, they don't have anything to do with punk rock. Or fat kids. Or desperate homeless musicians. They look like a couple from a magazine. The woman's wearing a short, pressed black skirt and high heels. She has long legs and she's wearing black stockings with a seam down the back. Her blond hair is cut like a *Vogue* model and I think she's hot. I wonder if that's what I'm supposed to see. Is this another elaborate plot to make me horny then promise me the world?

The man leans forward and laughs. He is what the magazines would refer to as "chiseled." He's got brown hair, cut close, and he's wearing a brown leather jacket—the kind with a belt that ties at the waist. When he laughs, his cheekbones move just like they're supposed to. His cheeks don't puff because they're nonexistent. They're sculpted lines rather than balloons. *I hate him.* If Curt thinks watching two perfect, skinny people eat is going to change my mind about being his drummer he's crazier than I thought.

"Curt," I say, "this is ridiculous. I'm sick of watching these people. They're perfect, all right? Is that what you want me to see?" Despite the waitress, I want to pay the bill and get out of there.

Curt shakes his head. "You're not watching them," he says. "You're watching *you*. If you'd watch *them* you'd see it." He takes out a handful of pills and lines them up behind his napkin. There are red, yellow, green, and blue ones. A regular rainbow of pharmaceuticals. He catches me staring and makes an exasperated head motion toward the couple.

Their food arrived fifteen minutes ago, but they're not nearly done eating. I wish they'd hurry up. The woman only has an omelet with some kind of vegetable in it and the man ordered the pasta. They're talking a lot and they both eat slow and sexy like people on television. The woman sits on a barstool with her legs crossed and takes one bite every two minutes. She chews carefully, as if she doesn't want anyone to see her swallow. The man does the same thing, only worse. He stops altogether for long periods of time and says things that make the woman tilt her head back and laugh.

I roll my eyes. They're both super skinny, so in my opinion they should just eat and be done with it. What the hell do they have to worry about?

"Fucking twigs from hell," I say, just to be contrary. And it's sort of true because they're pretty dull to watch. All they do is take turns tossing their heads back ceremoniously.

Curt nods and takes a bottle of NyQuil from a fold inside his shirt. He drinks about a third of it, and I glance over at him.

"Is that such a good—?"

"Are you *watching*?!" Curt interrupts. "You're not going to see anything if you don't watch. Watch how they fucking *eat*. Think how you feel when you eat like that."

Well, that's easy, I think. *I don't ever eat like that, except when I'm in public and I'm nervous about people watching me. Like when we went to Dad's retirement dinner. . . .* I pause.

The woman pushes the remains of her omelet around her plate, and the man takes a forkful of pasta. I've watched them take a hundred bites already, but this time I notice the way the woman glances at the cook, at her reflection in the window, at the door. . . . I notice the fact that the man still has his jacket tied even though they've been sitting there for half an hour. I notice the small run starting just above the heel of the woman's shoe.

I look at Curt, but he has his head down on the booth, so I narrow my eyes and keep watching.

Then I see it.

I see it out of the corner of my eye as the man moves his fork toward his mouth. He's talking to the woman and he looks like the same pompous asshole I've been watching for the last hour. Truly. Then he moves the fork and a piece of pasta falls off. It hits his lip and smears cheese down his perfect, clefted chin. He tries to act cool, but for a split second, like a flash of light, I see what he's hiding.

Curt looks up with his chin still on the table. He's watching me watch them. "You saw it, didn't you?" he breathes.

I shake my head. "No. I didn't see anything really. . . ." I squint.

The woman puts a small amount of egg on her fork, then lifts it tentatively. She's trying to act beautiful, in control. She moves her body sideways, then opens her mouth. . . .

"See?" Curt asks, drowsy. "You see it?"

I stare, fascinated. Maybe, after all, I do.

Curt nods in answer to the question I haven't asked.

"Finally," he says. "Do you get it now?"

I nod very slowly. The woman takes another bite, and I don't think about her legs anymore. I just watch for the flash. I don't think I will, but I see it again. One minute she looks confident, perfect, the next I see something else. I cringe.

I try watching the man instead, but that's worse. I realize for the first time that he's trying *really* hard.

Curt watches me watch them.

"I knew you'd see it," he says. "Okay, now stop looking."

71.

I FEEL LIKE I'VE JUST SEEN someone murdered. Or maybe I've found salvation. I don't know which.

Curt sneezes again and blows his nose loudly. His eyes are cloudy and he leans back in the booth as if it's propping him up. I give a small, involuntary shake.

"Curt," I say, very solemn, "what has this got to do with me being your drummer?"

I should be able to make this connection; in fact, I think I already have made the connection, but I need to hear him say it. Curt closes his eyes. He's silent, and for a moment I've lost him. Then he sniffs. He tries to sit up. Looks at me.

"That moment . . . ," he says at last. His voice is mellow and gravelly. It trails off, then starts again.

"That moment when you see through the bullshit?" he says a moment later. "That's what punk music is all about. That's what *anything* great is all about. We're all just stuffing our faces, no matter what we look like, and people need to figure that out. When you can *play* that moment, you've got it."

He's just revealed the secret truth of Curt MacCrae. Maybe something larger than that. If I were Curt, I would weep. I would press my skinny cheek against the cool table and let the tears roll into my soup.

I huff three times, rapid and loud.

"And me?" I choke.

Curt smiles. He leans down and presses his skinny cheek onto the cool table.

"You live that moment," he says.

72.

FAT KID CRYING IN DINER.

It's stupid that I'm crying. I'm not doing it loud or anything. I don't even think Curt notices because his eyes are closed. But the tears keep running down my cheeks. I feel them on my lips and my fat tongue reaches out to lick them off.

73.

WE'RE STANDING OUTSIDE watching traffic and my

mind is spinning. It's cold out, but the cold makes me alive. The sounds of the city are loud, intense. Horns, voices, music somewhere in the distance. Life has shrunk to the size of this time and this place. Me. Curt. A second chance.

The implications are staggering. I stare at each person walking by and imagine the moment they open their mouths, forks poised in midair. I picture them licking ice-cream cones, tongues extended.

Some of this makes me happy. Insanely happy. A short Spanish woman walks by and I picture her eating a taco and practically get tears in my eyes. I see an old man with massive age spots and imagine him eating something forbidden, like a vanilla cream–filled Dunkin' Donut. I imagine the way the cream would spurt all over his face and how he probably wouldn't be able to chew it, so there'd be food spilling down his chin, but he wouldn't care because he'd be happy and when you're old no one expects you to have a facade. I imagine myself as that old man.

I look up and my eyes land on one of those giant billboards. A half-naked woman leans seductively over a shiny new car. She's incredibly sexy, a babe with cleavage wearing a red string, and I imagine her leaning forward, toward me, beckoning. But just when I'm getting into that vision, a vanilla cream–filled donut comes flying out of nowhere, like a spaceship. It flies to her and I imagine her taking a bite. I'm trying hard to keep her sexy, but it doesn't work. Now she looks stupid bent over the car with her breasts sticking out of her bikini top. No one can eat a Dunkin' Donut like that.

"Oh, man," I whisper. "Oh, man, oh, man, oh, man."

I turn to Curt, to ask him if he thinks this is some kind of new perversion—Fat Kid porn. But when I turn around he's not there. I make a half circle, then see him at my feet. While I've been contemplating the universe, he's very quietly passed out.

74.

THE FIRST THING I DO is panic.

FAT KID GETS HYSTERICAL. Do not pass Go. Do not collect two hundred dollars.

I kneel beside Curt and huff loudly. I shake him, but I'm afraid I'll crush him if I grip too hard. He's bony and hollow through all the layers of clothes. When I touch his skin it's hot, like a flame. I start to sweat and pound on Curt's chest and a passerby stops and asks if I need help.

"Should I call nine-one-one?" the woman asks. She doesn't step too close, just leans forward as if Curt might be contagious.

"Yes," I holler. "Call nine-one-one. No, wait . . . yes, okay." I'm hyperventilating. My fat fingers press into Curt's face and I pry his eyes open. They're white and empty. I start to shake.

A jogger hands me his water bottle. "Try this," he says just as I'm about to start CPR. I don't know how to do CPR, but I've seen it done in the movies. I stare at the water bottle, wondering what to do with it as I consider the fact that I was about to put all my weight onto Curt's twig ribs.

"Splash it in his face," the jogger says. "If he's passed out, the water might wake him up."

Not a bad alternative to crushing someone's rib cage.

I open the pop-top and throw the water hard. Curt sputters and his eyes open a quarter of the way. He makes a noise that's unintelligible, so I shake him again.

"You fucker," I yell. My fat cheeks flap. "What did you take? What the hell did you take?" The NyQuil bottle has rolled out of his shirt onto the sidewalk. I keep shaking him and Curt keeps sputtering. I look up and there are a lot of people watching.

"What the fuck are you staring at?!" I yell. I don't think about it. The words just come out. Only later do I think, *I waited my whole life to yell that, and I didn't even enjoy it.*

75.

WE'RE IN THE CAB and Curt is groggy. He's slurring something about legitimate over-the-counter pharmaceuticals, but I'm unconvinced. I recognized Imodium, NyQuil, Tylenol, maybe a decongestant or an antihistamine . . . but what were the blue ones?

"I'm taking you to the hospital," I announce. I've instructed the driver to take us to Union Medical. Curt sits up and shakes his head.

"*Nowayman. I'llgetout. Gotnoinsurance* . . ." He leans toward the cab door and attempts to open it, but he's too weak. We're at a light, but it scares me anyway and I reach over to pull him back. I pull too hard and his body flops like a rag doll. His head lolls against the seat.

"You've got a fever," I say, breathing loud. "You need a doctor."

Curt curls up.

"*Can'twejustgotoyourhouse?*" he slurs. "*S'jussacold. Wegottapracticeforthenextgig.*"

I want to give in. Truly I do. I want to go home so Dad can fix this. But there's no way I'm giving in. Not this time. This time Curt doesn't win.

"Hang in there," I say. "We're almost there."

76.

THE EMERGENCY ROOM IS PACKED. There are people everywhere. Bleeding, moaning, sick people. The place smells like a battle between vomit and Lysol with vomit clearly winning. The fluorescent lights are so bright they make everything look gray.

I plow through the crowd, knowing we look like something out of a *Twilight Zone* episode. Huge pounding Fat Kid and a walking corpse. Curt shuffles behind me, bent over like an old man, complaining that he's tired and he'll be arrested. He tells me they'll call his mom and his stepfather will answer and then he'll have to hate me because really he's fine since the medicine he took is doing just what it's supposed to do. He says this twice, as if I'm the one whose view of reality is distorted. Why can't I see that this is exactly what was supposed to happen?

I reach the main desk and try to flag a nurse's attention. They ignore me. The one time in my life I don't want to be overlooked and everyone is intent on something else. Curt slides down the wall and I prop him up with my foot.

Goddamn it, I think. *Somebody see me.* A doctor runs past as a gurney surrounded by EMTs slides through the hospital's double doors. I hear the words "gunshot wound" and "two more on the way." I'm standing in the midst of chaos and every one of these people is hurting. Some of them won't make it. My eyes must be huge.

I call Dad from the pay phone, collect. He answers and I hear the television in the background. I hear Dayle laughing and imagine the two of them sitting together watching some game, eating chips. I almost feel guilty, but I'm so scared I can't think straight.

"Dad," I say, "Curt's sick. We're at the emergency room, but they're not admitting him. . . ." I choke. "He's passed out on the floor . . ."

I mean to say more, but Dad doesn't make me. I hear the control settle into his tone, and know he's going to take care of things. It's going to be all right. He asks me the name of the hospital and where our location is. I almost hear him glance at his watch.

"Okay," he says. "It's twenty-one-hundred hours. I'll be at your location in twenty-seven minutes. Understand? Hold your spot and I'll be right there. Keep trying to get a doctor's attention. Do whatever you need to do to get a doctor's attention."

I nod even though I know he can't hear me.

"Okay, Dad. I will. I will, Dad. I'll do it. . . ."

I keep talking long after he's hung up the phone.

77.

I'M A SIX-FOOT-ONE, three-hundred-pound teenager with no clue how to get someone's attention when I really need it. I stare at everyone who walks by, but no one is looking at me. *No one is looking at me.* I almost laugh but the situation is so completely not funny that I think I might cry instead. Finally, I've had enough.

I plant myself in the doorway between the nurses' station and the waiting room and become THE FAT KID WALL. There is no getting past me. I cross my arms and refuse to move.

A nurse glares as she tries to get through. She's holding a chart and she snaps at me.

"Get out of the way!"

I can tell she wants to push me aside, but thinks twice about the idea. She looks frazzled.

"My friend needs help," I say, and the nurse looks around as if I'm lying. I point at Curt and she looks at him without leaning down, then turns back to me.

"Have you filled out the paperwork?" she asks. "We have to take people in a certain order and right now I've got two gunshot wounds coming and a head trauma, so why don't you fill out the paperwork and we'll admit your friend as soon as we can."

I start to sputter, but force myself to swallow hard.

"He needs someone to look at him now," I say. "I can't fill out the paperwork because I don't know the answers and no one's coming who does know the answers, so why don't you just look at him now."

The nurse shakes her head. She hates me, and that's a shame because she's a perfect blond with a ponytail and lacquered nails. She frowns, but when I won't move she has no choice. She leans down and props Curt's head against the wall. She feels his forehead and opens his eyes.

"What did he take?" she asks. I move away from the door and crouch next to her. I really don't know and I say as much. The nurse rolls her eyes. She looks up and calls over the counter. "Dan, I need an IV and a gurney for this one. . . ."

78.

I SIT BY MYSELF in the waiting area. They've taken Curt somewhere and I wasn't allowed to go with him. They wheeled him out as if it were an imposition, a sacrifice they were making on my behalf. They didn't even see him. I want to sit on them. Pin them to the ground and tell them he's the best guitarist they'll ever meet. Instead I do nothing but wait.

And think about Mom.

Now that I'm sitting here with nothing to do I can't stop the single thought that's been trying to surface all evening. *Last time I was here was the day Mom died.* I was a skinny kid sitting in the waiting room with my little brother, watching for Dad. We'd been in her room together, but when she coded, the doctors made Dayle and me leave. Dayle was petrified. He held my hand so tight the circulation stopped and when I tried to let go he started to shake. I kept saying, "Everything will be all right. She'll be fine. I promise."

But she wasn't.

And I wasn't. And he wasn't.

I wish Dad would arrive. I stare at the double doors willing him to walk through, and it feels like hours before they finally slide open. Then I see him. My dad. And behind him, my little brother.

Dad looks stoic, as always, but Dayle looks almost as scared as he did nine years ago. He looks like a kid who doesn't know what's going on, and I finally figure out that's what he is. I want to say something to him. To apologize for never seeing that before. For telling him everything would be fine, then acting like it was for everyone but me. But when they reach me Dad goes pale.

"Curt?" he asks when he sees I'm alone. I concentrate on breathing slow.

"I don't know," I say. "They took him in a while ago and told me to wait here. It hasn't been very long, but—"

Dad doesn't wait. He strides to the nurses' station and leans far over the counter. I can't hear what's being said but after a few minutes a nurse comes around and says, "Right this way." Dayle doesn't say much, but he follows Dad too closely, almost stepping on his heels.

The three of us head down a long empty corridor. When we reach Curt he's in one of the cubicles. He has an IV hooked up and a tube up his nose. They have him dressed in one of those paper hospital gowns and I wonder what happened to his clothes. I remember the look on his face when Dad threw them out and hope they haven't thrown them away again. I keep thinking about the clothes as if that will prevent me from thinking about Curt's body.

When I look at him I see *skinny* instead of skinny. His arms are outside the blankets, unearthed from the layers of clothing that usually hide them. They're black-and-blue bones. He's a twisted sparrow that's flown into a window.

Dayle and I hang back, but Dad sits down next to Curt. He touches his forehead, and Curt's eyes half open.

"*Igotafever*," he mumbles. My father nods.

"That you do," he says. "What did you take for it?"

Curt shrugs. Or he would shrug if he could move his shoulders. "Some stuff," he says quietly. "*Lotsofstuff*."

My father's jaw tightens, but he keeps his hand on Curt's forehead.

"You took lots of stuff?" he repeats. He's gentle, the way I remember him being when Dayle and I were little kids. Curt nods almost imperceptibly.

"Why would you do that?" Dad asks.

The question is simple, but Curt's eyes move back and forth between Dad and me. He looks tired and confused.

" 'Cause," he says, as if it's obvious, "*didn'tfeelwell.*"

79.

I LOOK UP CURT'S MOM'S NUMBER and we try to get her on the phone. When his stepfather answers, Dad hangs up. I see him standing at the pay phone without moving, one hand still holding the receiver. Dad's studying the mottled floor tiles and I can see what he's thinking.

I almost say, *"You did the right thing,"* but don't. I do, however, mentally remove the word "dysfunctional" from the blue light sign flashing above Dad's head. I turn to my brother.

"Come on, Dayle," I say. "It's time to go. Dad'll stay with Curt."

We take a cab home, and when we get there the apartment is quiet. And empty. I look around for Dad even though I know he's not here. We turn on all the lights and make sandwiches in the kitchen. I'm tired and starving, but Dayle looks shaky. He's hardly said two words all night, and now he kicks at the table leg and eats in huge, gulping bites.

"You okay?" I ask.

He rolls his eyes as if I'm a moron. Snorts. "Yeah. Why wouldn't I be? I don't care what happens to Curt. He's *your* friend. . . ."

He stabs at his sandwich with the mustard knife, and I don't say anything at first, but then I nod. "That's true," I say, "but Curt really likes you. He said you should be our roadie when Rage/Tectonic gets famous. Thinks you've got potential."

Dayle stops stabbing the sandwich, but looks suspicious.

"He said that?"

"Yeah," I say. "Curt acts like he doesn't notice people, but he liked you from the beginning. He invited you to the gig, didn't he?"

Dayle pauses.

"Well . . ."

"Dayle," I say, as if it's an afterthought, "there are people who like you even when you're not winning sports trophies. You know that, don't you? Me, Curt, Dad . . . Mom loved you, too. Maybe you don't remember, but she was crazy about you from the moment you were born. If she were here she'd tell you that." It's probably the most important thing I've ever said to my brother. I keep going as if it's no big deal, but I know it's a big deal. It would be to me. "Trust me," I say. "Curt likes you."

Dayle bites his lip. "Well, I always thought Curt was cool, it's just that I didn't think you guys wanted me around. . . ."

I don't make him finish.

"I always want you around. You're my brother."

In our entire lives I've never said this to him. I've spent years waiting for those exact words and it never once occurred to me to give them away.

80.

I WAKE UP IN THE MORNING and remember something's wrong. I can't remember what it is right away, then it comes back to me. Curt's in the hospital. Dad's with him. Dayle's scared. I'm . . . For once I do not define myself. I get out of bed, shower, and dress in a pair of tan pants and a T-shirt that reads ALBUQUERQUE. I wake up Dayle.

"I'm going to the hospital," I tell him.

He's mostly asleep, so I accept the half nod I get in response, then write a note and leave it on the counter. I call a cab and wait for it outside.

When it arrives, I slide in and tell the driver my destination. The cab smells like cigarette smoke even though the sticker on the back panel reads NO SMOKING. I roll down the window and try to breathe only fresh air. I want to suck it in before I reach the hospital. I'm starting all over again and I want a fresh start. This time around I don't have room for pollution. I lean forward and breathe, watching the city move past my open window. Today, I fit. I'm just one more anonymous person in a yellow cab.

I take a deep breath. *This is where it begins,* I think.

Fat Kid Breathing in a Cab.

81.

CURT'S BEEN MOVED to a real room, just he and an old guy wheezing away in the other bed. I find Dad with the curtain drawn, sitting beside Curt. He looks up when I arrive, and I think we both realize this scene is familiar. Dad is composed even though I know he stayed up all night. Guard duty. Dad's good at that. I'd smile if he didn't look so grim.

"How's Curt?" I ask, nodding at the pile of blankets in the bed. I wouldn't know it was Curt if Dad weren't sitting there. Curt's lost under the paper-thin hospital blankets. The top of his head barely emerges and his hair is matted back from sweat or grime. Maybe both. Dad sighs.

"He'll be okay," he says. "Tonight was tricky, but he's sleeping now. He's got pneumonia and took too much medication for it. He's malnourished and a bit bruised." He pauses, then looks at me.

"Do you know how he got those bruises?" he asks. I shake my head. I don't, and the truth is, he could've gotten them anywhere. Fight, accident, stepfather, thrashing, throwing himself into a drum set . . . I don't really know what Curt does to survive. I don't know how he lives or where he goes, if he has any friends aside from me and the Puppets. I shake my head again, and Dad nods as if he understands.

"I talked to his mom," he offers. He glances at Curt to make sure he's not awake. I start to feel hopeful because Curt always talks about his mom as if she's the decent one. Maybe when she hears he's in the hospital she'll kick the asshole out and let Curt back in.

"Yeah?" I say. "When's she coming?"

Dad's silent for a long time. His face is as still and solemn as granite. "She's not," he says at last.

I'm confused, thinking he must mean she's not coming *right away*. I fill in the words he forgot to say. Then it hits me.

"She's not coming?" I repeat. I picture the woman I saw entering the apartment building—the one with the tired eyes and splattered uniform. "What do you mean she's not coming? Did you speak to her? Not the ass—not his stepfather, but *her*? Did you tell her he's in the freaking hospital?"

Dad looks at me and it's one of the many occasions when I wish I knew what he was thinking. He looks the way he looked right after my mother died, when there was something he wanted to say, but couldn't say it. He coughs.

"Yes, I told her," he says. He studies Curt's monitors as if he's making sure nothing's changed. "I spoke to her directly and she's not coming."

I sit down in the chair opposite my father. I plunk down all three hundred pounds of me as if I'm made of cement. The chair groans, but I don't think about it. I just stare ahead as if someone died. It shouldn't be such a big deal, I tell myself. I bet Curt would pretend it wasn't a big deal. But for some reason that doesn't make me feel better. It *is* a big deal.

"How can a mother refuse to visit her kid in the hospital? What if he died?! I bet she'd be sorry then. . . ."

I don't mean to, but my voice rises and I pound my fist into the bed. Curt doesn't move, but his heart monitor beeps faster. Dad glances at it, then reaches over and puts his large leathery fist on top of mine. I draw in a quick breath and Dad lets go of my hand. He starts talking the way he used to talk after the funeral. Slow, steady, calm.

"Sometimes," he says, "people give up on each other. They don't mean to, but things happen. . . ."

There's a long silence.

"In the military," Dad starts again, "we teach our boys to go the distance. Just like I tried to teach you and Dayle. A soldier never gives up until they've reached their objective. Perseverance." Dad pauses. "But in wartime," he says, "it's easy to remember because there's a war to be fought and you have to fight it. You give it one hundred percent because your life depends on it. In civilian life it's not that easy and sometimes people give up too soon. It doesn't mean they stop loving each other, but maybe they stop trying so hard and let things slide when they ought to hang on tight. Maybe they don't tunnel through the mud because they think they don't have to, or they get tired. . . ."

My father is tunneling through the mud. I close my eyes.

"Dad," I say, "she shouldn't have given up on him. Curt's a great guitarist. He's funny and he tries really hard to make people like him, and he taught me about other people and eating, and about seeing stuff that's hidden. . . ." I pause and think very carefully about what I'm about to say.

"You never gave up on us like that," I say. "You didn't give up on Mom, and you've never given up on me. You haven't given up on Curt and he's not even your kid. It's not your fault I got fat. I know that, Dad."

For the first time I name what's unspoken between us, and Dad has to fight hard to keep his stoic expression. He looks away, but at the same time reaches out and takes my hand, this time with no pretense.

We sit there for a long time. The shades in the room are drawn and it's dim, shadowed. Noises from the hallway drift inside, but Dad and I are silent together. When he finally stands up, I wish he wouldn't go.

"I'll be back this evening," Dad says. "The nurses will be around in the afternoon, and Curt will probably wake up for a while. He'll be glad to see you."

Dad hands me some money.

"Get yourself some lunch and call me if anything changes." He pauses at the door.

"And Troy?" he says. I turn around.

"Yeah, Dad?"

"Proud."

82.

CURT WAKES UP A LITTLE after lunchtime. He's groggy and asks for my dad. When I tell him Dad went home he asks for chocolate pudding. He's barely awake and he can't sit up; he's on a diet of ice chips, but he's convinced he could eat chocolate pudding if someone just gave it to him.

"Damn," he whispers when I tell him they're all out. "What are the chances?"

He tries to fall back asleep, but shifts uncomfortably. His blankets twist into spirals and his eyes stay half shut. He moans only when the nurse comes in . . . says his chest hurts, his back hurts, everything hurts. . . . She falls for it every time. She gives him more pain medication, and he drifts in and out, talking when I least expect it.

"Don't forget about the gig," he says after waking up in a panic. Once he says, "Ten dollars. That's just ten dollars. A bargain for what you're getting."

Listening to him makes me wonder if this will end up as one of his songs. If it does I bet it will be a song about rage, bedpans, and a thousand distorted nurse faces. I bet it will be about feeling tired and sick and not getting chocolate pudding when it's the one thing in the world you truly want.

83.

BY TUESDAY AFTERNOON Curt's doing better. I visit after school and find him sitting up in bed watching *Love Boat* reruns. There's a pile of used tissues making a pyramid on the floor beside him, and an empty food tray lies abandoned nearby. An alarm is going off down the hall and the room smells like piss. The guy in the next bed rasps every time he breathes. It's putrid.

Curt grins, oblivious, and points to the television.

"I lub de *Love Boadt*," he says. "Whad a show. Gopher's de besdt." He blows his nose loudly. "I've been wadtching the besdt shows all day. *Love Boadt, Gilligan's Island, Three's Company*." He's blissfully happy. And nasal.

I sit down in the blue plastic chair and try to remember what he looked like on stage, but can't conjure that image in relation to this person in the hospital gown. Not because he's sick, but because he's so happy.

"How you doing?" I ask.

Curt nods appreciatively. "T," he says, "this is the besdt place I've ever been." He rubs his eyes. "Look . . ." He presses a button and after a minute a nurse comes in.

"Hi," he says. She shakes her head.

"Curt, what have we told you about the buzzer?"

"You wanna meedt my friend T?" he asks.

The nurse smiles. She's petite with cherry-red hair and perfect, round breasts.

"Hi, T," she says, then gives Curt a mock glare. "Rest," she orders.

Curt smiles, satisfied. He leans back and puts his hands behind his head like one of those rich men in the movies. Nods at me knowingly.

"They're here all the time, you know," he tells me. "All you've got to do is push the button."

84.

TWO DAYS LATER Curt's trying to sleep, sweating like he's in a sauna. The television's off, but he still looks happy. He grins when he sees me and motions toward the chair beside his bed. I flop down next to him.

"Know what I like about this place?" he asks without preamble. I shake my head, and Curt's eyes dart around the room.

"There are so many people around," he says. "There's this guy"— he jerks his head at the guy in the next bed—"and the nurses and doctors. Ollie came to visit me and he said Piper's coming tomorrow. Maybe Mike . . . and your dad's here a lot. Oh, wait . . ." He gets excited and tries to sit up, but doesn't. "I've got great news. We've got another gig. This Saturday."

He waits for my reaction, but I hesitate.

"You think you'll be out of here by Saturday?" I ask. Curt doesn't miss a beat.

"Are you fucking insane? Of course I won't be out of here by Saturday. I have *pneumonia*." He drags the word out like he's talking to a kid. "But," he says, "we can't let a little thing like me being hospitalized stand in the way of our second big debut. We're gonna kick ass. Oh," he adds, "and I've invited all the nurses."

"Curt," I say, "I think maybe we should wait until you're better. I mean, it won't be that long before you're out and then we'll set up a show. . . ."

Curt scoffs.

"It will be a *long time*," he says, "because I'm *sick* and they have to let me stay until I get better." He tries to punch me in the arm but can't reach. "Don't worry," he says. "You've got all the nervous stuff behind you now. Or maybe you could do it again and it could be your trademark." He thinks about this idea and I can tell he's lik-

ing it. I would object, but the nurse comes in to take his temperature.

The nurse is a young guy, probably in his twenties, and he's
wearing green scrubs like the people on television. He reads the ther-
mometer, throws away the plastic covering, and frowns.

"I don't get it," he mutters. "We've already put you on new
meds . . ." Curt nods gravely as the nurse hands him a small paper
cup with his pain pills in it. Curt swallows them, or at least I think
he does. As soon as the nurse leaves he rolls the pills out from under
his tongue and spits them out. He reaches over to the houseplant
on his bed stand and casually buries them beneath the dirt. Then he
unhooks his IV and squeezes out some of his antibiotic. He rehooks
the IV, all the while continuing our discussion as if nothing unusual
is happening.

"So, Saturday night I'll sneak out, which won't be a big deal because I've been figuring out their shifts and so long as Mr. Death
Rattle over there doesn't decide to kick off, I can make it. . . ."

I stare with my mouth open. "What are you doing?!" I finally
demand, wondering if I really saw him do what I think I saw him do.
My cheeks puff and I'm sure I look like someone just got murdered.
Curt stops. He gives me an innocent look, which turns into a glare
when I don't respond appropriately.

"Relax," he says, nodding at the television. "Don't freak out.
There's plenty left. Plenty."

"And the pills?"

He scratches his head. "Those are for *later,* when I can't get them
all the time. This place is loaded. I'm just saving a few of my own and
borrowing some, uh . . . *eh-hem.*"

My eyes bug out and I stare at the plant, wondering how many
pills—and *whose* pills—he's buried underneath the red blossoms. I
want to tell him he's insane, but I don't.

"So," I ask, "how long do you think you'll be sick? What'll you do when you get better?"

Curt scrunches his nose. Sneezes. He ignores my first question entirely and answers the second.

"Form a band. With you. Whaddaya think?"

I try to laugh, but it comes out as a cross between a snort and a huff.

"No," I say, "I'm serious. Where will you go? Where were you sleeping before you got sick? After I blew the gig?"

Curt freezes. His eyes narrow and his jaw sets tight.

"What's up with you?" he asks. He's looking at me like I'm fat and I start to hyperventilate, then remind myself this is serious.

"Nothing's up," I say. "I just wondered, you know, you've got those bruises and—"

Curt lets out a loud laugh. Too loud.

"What are you, the CIA, or something? You think you've got to know everything about my life?"

Curt laughs again, but he doesn't really think it's funny. Then he snaps.

"Well, fuck off."

He's never told me to fuck off before. Even when he was pissed during practice he never meant it. But this time I think he means it. I can tell by the set of his eyes. I have two options. I can ignore everything about his life he doesn't want me to see or I can fuck off. Simple as that.

One month ago it would've been simple, but now I'm not so sure.

85.

I SIT IN THE LOBBY for a long time weighing my options. I ought to go home, but I'm restless and my brain is spinning, so I call Ollie instead. I tell myself I just want to pound something, pick up the sticks and beat the crap out of the drum set, but as soon as I arrive at The Dump I know that's not why I'm here.

I've got to make a choice, but before I do I have to know what I'm choosing between. I've never once sat on this stage and played the way I think I can play. In fact, I haven't even been back since the eruption. I expect everything to look different. Humiliating. But it doesn't.

I walk in and the place is almost empty. Someone's setting up the bar and Ollie's on stage setting up the drums. He asks about Curt, but I don't feel like talking about Curt, so all I do is grunt. Ollie doesn't push me. He turns up the music as loud as it will go, grabs one set of sticks, and throws me the other.

I climb onto the stage and take the empty place behind the set. It feels good—the way I wanted it to feel. A release. The bass pounds, *womp, womp,* deep in my gut, and the smack of the sticks feels sweet against the skins. Ollie uses everything in sight as his set and makes sounds I never dreamed of. I love listening to him, and at first I let him lead, but then I think, *Fuck that.* I'm remembering what Curt said about great drummers adding to the conversation. Now I've finally got something to say. I'm furious and I let myself play that way. I'm a distorted grotesque parody of a teenager who never saw anything beyond himself, and I decide to play like one. I think about everything that's happened in the last nine years, about Dad and Dayle, and Curt's stupid, self-destructive ultimatum. I play until I'm dripping sweat and my arms ache, but I don't stop.

I want to play forever.

Ollie and I bounce off each other's rhythms, and once when I look up I see the bartender nodding, slapping the counter with his spill rag. I think, *This is what it's all about.* More than anything, I want this feeling to last. I want a shot at being on stage, not in the crowd but *on stage,* saying everything that's in my distorted, fat brain. I want every one of my twisted ideas exposed for the world to see. The thought that I might never get that chance makes my stomach turn. It's like I've been in prison my whole life and the day I'm set free they close the world.

We play for over an hour before the music breaks and when I finally set down the drumsticks I'm breathing hard, but it still kills me to stop. I keep thinking, *This is the last time you'll sit here. That bartender is the only person who will ever hear you play like this, on stage, unfettered.* I tell myself it doesn't have to work this way. I can choose not to confront Curt and go on stage Saturday night while I've still got the guts. Curt will sneak out of the hospital just like he said and we'll play our gig. Maybe someone would sign us, and *then* Curt could get better. . . .

But deep down I know that's not what will happen. Weatherman says optimism is unlikely—there's only a five percent chance of happy endings. No one would sign us, Curt wouldn't get better, and the thought of sitting on stage without him is worse than not sitting on stage at all.

I swing my legs over the throne and wipe my palms on my pants.

"Thanks for letting me play," I tell Ollie. That's when I notice him grinning. He's watching me, twirling a drumstick between his fingers.

"You know," he tells me, "that set was freakin' awesome. You keep this up and Rage/Tectonic will be huge. *You'll* be huge." He pauses. "No pun intended."

It's a cool compliment, but I only smile weakly.

"Of course, you'll have to get Curt out of the goddamn hospital," he continues, "and convince him you're not going to bail again, but that shouldn't be hard. Once he sees you play like *this* . . . man, T. You'll have the world on a platter."

I stop midstride. *The World On A Platter.* It's an odd thing to say to a fat kid, but now that he's said it I wonder if he's right. What if I could have everything I want? Order everything on the menu for a change? I want to play the drums. I'm positive about that. But I also want a friend. A healthy one. I'm positive about that, too. I look up.

"You know something, Ollie?" I say. "I think you might be on to something."

86.

I'VE BEEN THINKING ABOUT IT all night, and I think I've got one shot at making things right.

Saturday morning I take the long walk to Curt's room, hoping I can pull this off. I find him eating hospital macaroni and cheese and chocolate pudding and he's really happy about it in a tired sort of way. Every time he opens his mouth it's like I'm looking at a gaping chasm of tired happiness and I have to turn my eyes. I stare at the pictures on the walls instead. Sierra desert. Still life of a mango.

"You cool?" he asks me.

"Yeah," I say. "I'm cool."

"Good," Curt says as if it's settled, "because this is going to work out perfect. This gig's bigger than the last one. Full set. We'll play the three songs we've practiced, that way the crowd will be primed and if the other ones aren't as good we can cruise on adrenaline. I've been taking my medication all day and I feel most excellent."

He stops. "You know," he ponders, "there may be reps in the audience tonight. If there are we'll know it. You can always tell because they're just a little too straight. And old. Man, they're almost always old."

He pauses, waiting for me to say something. When I don't he picks up where he left off.

"So we'll play the gig, then I'll sneak back here and pretend like nothing's happened. I'll act like I was taking a walk or something. I love taking walks around this place. You get to wear your pajamas all day. Walk around bare ass and no one cares. Sweet."

I still haven't said anything. I'm picturing Curt, half his ass hanging out, picking the locks on all the hospital medicine cabinets, making absurd deals with shifty orderlies, maybe sneaking into rooms and liberating old people of their narcotics . . . Curt's oblivious. He takes another bite of chocolate pudding and toys with the remote control. All the seventies reruns flash by like a retrospecial on fast-forward. I take a deep breath.

"Listen," I say, "I was thinking you shouldn't keep your medications here. What if someone decides to water your plant? It's starting to look a little droopy, don't you think?" Curt frowns and inspects the plant closely. It *is* looking kind of wilted. "I was thinking I could take them to The Dump and you could take care of them tonight. Stash them somewhere after the show."

His face changes from worried to relieved, then back again. He hesitates.

"Yeah, I guess you could do that. . . ."

"Great. I'll take it now so nobody finds it before tonight's gig." I wipe the sweat off my forehead and Curt gives me a strange look. Yesterday he would have trusted me unconditionally, but today . . .

"Thanks, T," he says. "You're the best. I can always count on you."

I laugh nervously and lift the plant. I know I shouldn't rush this, but all I can think about is getting out the door.

"See ya later," I say. I want to say something else, something profound to prepare him for what I'm about to do, but I can't. Curt looks too happy. He stops me just as I reach the door.

"T," he says. "You can have my next chocolate pudding."

FAT KID GUILT WITH EXTRA WHIPPED CREAM.

87.

I'M JUDAS CARRYING A VERY healthy houseplant through the halls of Union Medical. It's the Fat Kid version of the Passion.

My hands are sweaty and the plant weighs a thousand pounds. I try to breathe normally but imagine everyone knows what I'm carrying and what I'm about to do. Half of them shake their heads thinking, *Why didn't you do this sooner?* The other half think, *You fucking moron—you're about to betray your only friend and give up the opportunity of a lifetime.* I can't decide who's right.

I carry the plant to the cafeteria, where I've arranged to meet Dad for lunch. I wind past the gift shop and through the halls until I smell the strange mixed odor of food and body fluids. Hospital cafeteria. I walk inside and wonder whether people think I'm a patient, there for some sort of medical treatment. A heart problem? Diabetes?

I balance the plant on one hip and scan the tables. I'm looking for Dad's polo shirt, but see Dayle's football jersey instead. He sees me and lifts one arm as if he might wave, then scratches his head. I carry the plant over and set it in front of him.

"What are you doing here?" I ask, surprised.

Dayle shrugs.

"Maybe I wanted to see how Curt was doing. . . ."

"Maybe?" I ask.

"Yeah," he says. "Maybe I was wondering."

I almost smile, but at that moment Dad walks up, carrying a tray with three sandwiches, Cokes, and desserts. He sets them down and doles out the food, oblivious to the houseplant that sits before us like a centerpiece.

"How's Curt?" Dad asks. "How's that new medication working out for him? Any better than the previous stuff?"

I shrug.

Dad unwraps his sandwich and takes a huge bite. He eats slowly and methodically, his chewing restrained, measured. I get the distinct impression he's enjoying the sandwich, and that makes me happy.

I look over at Dayle and he's eating with a purpose. He eats fast, and looks at Dad a lot. They have the same type of sandwich and I wonder if Dayle even likes his. I think he's trying so hard to be Dad, he might choke. I've never noticed this before, but I don't have time to think about it now.

I set my sandwich down, untouched, and take a deep breath.

"Dad," I say, "I think Curt needs some help. I think he should come live with us when he gets out of the hospital. . . ." I pause. "I think maybe part of why he's not getting better is because he doesn't have anywhere to go . . . afterward, I mean, and if he had a place to stay he could get better."

Dad stops midbite. Dayle keeps eating, but he watches me intently. I expect him to throw a fit, but for once he keeps quiet.

"What makes you say that?" Dad asks, but he doesn't ask as if he's asking for information. He asks as if it's a question about me.

I look from Dad to Dayle, then tip the houseplant over on the table.

"Oh, man," Dayle says. He stops with his mouth full, all his food wadded into one cheek. Half the pills Curt's supposed to have taken, along with dozens of pills he's obviously stolen, are now sitting in a clump of dirt in front of us.

I clear my throat.

"I think," I say, "Curt needs a place to stay."

Dad stares at the collection of pharmaceuticals in front of us, and I risk a glance at him.

"I also think you've considered the idea already, and I'm hoping you won't change your mind."

Dad's jaw is very tight and I hurry to make my case.

"I know what you're going to say," I huff. "You're going to tell me there are consequences to our actions, and if Curt's stealing medication he has to be reported to the authorities. You're going to tell me about responsibility, honesty, cause and effect. . . ." I pause. "And that's all good stuff. Stuff I believe in, but we both know the hospital will call the police, and we both know that Curt is over eighteen, and we both know that he's got talent if someone would just give him a chance. . . ."

Emotions pass over Dad's face like a shadow. He's thinking even before I start talking and before I say half my speech he reaches out and grabs my arm. His hand barely makes it around half of my bicep, but his fingers grip tight.

"You're asking me to lie," he says. He looks me right in the eyes. "You know that's what you're doing, don't you?"

I haven't thought of it that way, but I nod.

"I'm asking you to withhold strategic information," I offer.

Dad lets go of my arm. He runs both hands over his crew cut and glances around the cafeteria. It's mostly empty, but the little old lady two tables over stares at us like we're a traveling freak show. Dad glares until she turns away, then looks back at me.

"I know you want what's best for Curt," he says. "But what's best

174

for Curt is to get help. Curt *needs* help. Addiction to medication is still addiction. Stealing is still stealing."

Dad has a point—*I know it*—but I have a point, too.

"Yeah, Dad," I say, "but a jail term is still a jail term, and a criminal record is still a criminal record."

Dad and I have locked gazes and we barely remember Dayle is there until he clears his throat. My heart sinks. I think for sure he's going to say that I'm the king of the morons, and I'm humiliating him by defending my psycho, druggie friend and I can't afford to let his whining sway Dad's opinion.

"Dayle," I start, but my brother isn't saying what I thought he was going to say.

"If Curt goes to jail," he says, "he won't come back, will he?"

The question catches me off guard and I can't tell if Dayle thinks this is a good thing or a bad thing.

"I mean, if he thinks we turned him over to the police, or the doctors, or something, he might do whatever they make him do, but then he'll just go away and he won't have anyone like he has now."

Dad's lips form a thin line.

"Right now, Curt's got us," Dayle says. "And he's got Troy. . . ."

I stare at my brother like we've never met. He shrugs.

"I'm just saying it wouldn't do any good to turn him in, right? It wouldn't accomplish any *long-term objectives.* But you're pretty strict, Dad, and if he came and lived with us . . ."

I can't help it. I break into a huge grin. Dad's shoulders slump and I can tell he's melting.

"Little brother has a point," I say. "A good soldier keeps the long-term objectives foremost in his mind."

Dad gives me *the look.* Then he looks at Dayle. Dad may be glaring, but I almost think he wants to laugh. I almost think he wanted to be talked into this from the beginning. I'm about to say something else. Something about giving people chances and bending the rules every now and then so other people can fit through, but I don't think I have to. I suspect Dad already knows.

No one says a word for a full minute, then at last Dad looks up.

"What is it you want me to do?"

88.

I HAVE TO TELL CURT the news. It's four o'clock and he's wondering why I'm back. He keeps glancing behind me to see if I've brought him a change of clothes or something.

"You're not going to stay long, right?" he asks for the third time. I figure there's no use avoiding it any longer.

"Curt," I say at last, "we've got to talk." His eyes narrow, then widen.

"What?" he says. "Did they cancel? They cancelled on us?" He pauses, then glares in my direction. "Do not even tell me you're bailing out again. There is no way in hell after all I've put up with. . . ."

He's on a roll and I have to wave him off like one of those air-traffic controllers. "No," I spell out with huge, sweeping arm motions. "I'm not bailing, and they didn't cancel." I pause, take a deep breath. "My dad knows about the medications."

Curt's expression does one of those 180-degree slides where you see every thought that passes through a person's brain. His face goes from furious to blank.

"I gave him the plant . . . ," I say.

Blanker.

"He knows you were going to sneak out tonight. . . ."

He is completely and utterly vacant. I sigh.

"Curt," I say again, "I told Dad everything."

In the blink of an eye blank turns to terror. Terror turns to panic and Curt sits bolt upright, then moves to jump out of bed, but I place my huge body in front of him. He stops, settles back, and coughs, but his eyes dart around the room searching for an escape route.

"He's not going to call the cops," I say. "If you agree to get help he won't tell anyone about the pills. But you've got to come live with us. That's the deal."

I wait for his surprised relief, but it doesn't come. There's a long pause and I wonder if Curt really heard what I said. I want to shout, *I said you could come live with us,* but I don't. I watch Curt's eyes scanning the room for a way out, and when at last they land on me I involuntarily take a step back.

I recognize those eyes. *They're the eyes of someone standing just over the yellow line when the subway's coming. . . .*

Curt stares at the door, then starts to laugh. He laughs quietly at first, then louder, as if I'm playing the mother of all practical jokes and he's just figured it out. He laughs as if it's funny, but we both know it's not.

"You're trying to save me?" he says at last. "*You're* . . . trying to save . . . *me*?" He stops laughing and glares like he's accusing me of a crime. "No way," he says. "That's not how it goes. I told you that from the very beginning. I saved you, remember? I saved you."

I cringe. "Curt," I say, slowly and cautiously, "I'm offering you the deal of a lifetime. No rap sheet. No hospital authorities. No more living on the street. . . ."

Curt stops laughing and everything I thought he was melts away before my eyes. He doesn't fidget or cough. He's absolutely still.

"You can't do this," he says. He tries to look pleading, but it doesn't help.

"It's done," I say. Pleading turns to fury.

"You betrayed me?" he says. "We have our last best shot at a gig, you bail on me *again*, and you think it's the fucking deal of a lifetime?" He chokes. "Oh, man, T. The deal of a lifetime is a sweet gig on a Saturday night. It's a fucking cheese sandwich and chocolate pudding. It's a friend who doesn't fucking . . . fucking . . . turn you in to the . . ."

His face is red and he runs one bony hand through his hair.

"Curt," I say, "I haven't bailed on you. I'm right here. I told my dad about the pills because I wasn't going to let you *kill* yourself."

Curt doesn't even try to look at me.

"They weren't killing me," he says. "They were making me *feel better*. They were prescription. . . ."

He's getting louder and louder and every Fat Kid reflex in my body wants to bloat to the size of a helium balloon and float away, but I don't. I take a step closer.

"They weren't your prescription!"

My words ring out loudly and the tension in the room makes my chest constrict. I start to huff. I can feel Curt slipping out of my grasp. All this time I couldn't see and now it might be too late. I have to convince him that he can *do* this. I take a deep breath.

"You don't want to live here for the rest of your life," I say at last. It comes out as a whisper. "You don't want to run a low-grade temperature forever. . . ."

Curt refuses to look at me, but I waddle to the other side of the bed so he's forced to stare at my huge girth.

"Is that what you wanted?" I ask. I'm expecting him to tell me to fuck off again, but he doesn't. He bites his lip and twists the needle from his IV. His hands clutch the hospital blankets until his knuckles turn white.

"I wanted a week," he says at last. It comes out as a choked breath. "I wanted a week. Maybe two. I wanted a band when I got out. Those are things I could've had. I could've *had* that. . . ."

He chokes midsentence and sounds like he can't get enough air. There's sweat on his forehead and his nose is running. He's a fucking mess. I hand him a clump of Kleenex, forcing them into his fingers, but he drops them and runs his sleeve over his face.

"Curt," I say gently, "you still have a band. You have a band and a place to live if you'll just take them." I pause, but have to say it all. "You think no one else can see it, but your whole life is this convoluted series of lies. You talk about playing into that space, that space where there's nothing but real, but that's the only time you ever touch it. The rest of the time you're this big gaping wound you think no one else can see. You *pretend* everything, and then when someone doesn't go along with you it's time to bail *just in case. . . .* You think that's living?"

I know I should stop, but I don't.

"I may be this huge fat kid," I say, "but at least I know when I'm trying to put up a facade. At least I know when I'm failing miserably. At least I can accept help from someone who offers it instead of being so fucking scared that something might go right for a change."

I'm huffing loudly and I don't even care. "At least I don't look at people and use their vulnerability to manipulate them. At least I'm not *that* scared."

Curt closes his eyes.

"Take the deal, Curt," I say. I mean it. With every ounce of fat on my body, I mean it.

I wait for a long time, willing him to say yes, but Curt shakes his head.

"Why'd you have to tell him?" he says at last. "Why'd you have to do that?" His voice shakes. "You think you can have everything, *everything,* and just hand it over?" He wipes his nose. "Well, it doesn't work that way. How long do you think your dad will let me stay? Until you graduate? Go to college? How long until you get sick of the band? How long until you've sucked every moral lesson from this story and I'm left where I started?" He looks away. "Well, forget it. You don't get to save me, Troy. I told you that from the very beginning. You don't get to fucking save me. I saved you, remember? That's how I want it."

My heart pounds.

"Fine," I say. "Then you go to jail."

"Fine," says Curt.

Only it's not fine and we both know it. Curt is terrified and I'm sick.

"Dad won't pay your bail, you know. Ollie either. If the cops come they're going to put you in restraints until you're out of the hospital, then they're going to charge you with stealing . . . or possession . . . or something like that."

I'm trying to sound all technical, but Curt shrugs like it doesn't matter.

"Fine," he says. "If that's the way you want it. I knew you'd fucking bail on me. I knew it. . . ."

I want to throttle him, but I have one last card to play.

"What if I could prove to you that I'm not bailing? That no one's going to bail? What if I could show you everything you're giving up by being too chicken to take the deal? If I could do that, would you give me one chance?"

Curt scoffs.

"Yeah, right," he says. "And how exactly are you going to do that?"

I cross my arms over my chest.

"There's a lot about me you don't know, my friend." I tilt my head knowingly. "Don't mess with the Fat Kid."

89.

IT'S EXACTLY FIFTEEN MINUTES until show time and I'm backstage at The Dump staring into the audience like a maniac. I look like a psychopath, but that's not far from the truth, so I figure, *what the hell.* Everyone expects this to be a repeat of the Mount Vesuvius eruption, so the tension is thick. Piper and Mike keep walking past, shaking their heads. The girls jump every time I turn around. The stagehands make huge circles around me. They all think I've got stage fright, but it's worse than that. I'm still waiting for my guitarist to show up.

Five more minutes go by and Ollie comes over to peer around me.

"Think they're going to make it?" he asks for the tenth time in ten minutes.

I nod.

"They'll be here," I say. "I guarantee it."

I hope that I'm right. All those stories about Dad's glory days in the Marines, crossing enemy lines . . . What if he's lost his touch? What if he changed his mind and decided he won't take Curt out of the hospital without permission? He was pretty iffy about the whole scheme to begin with, but I thought I had him convinced. I thought . . .

Suddenly, the back door of The Dump swings open and there's Dad. He nods at me, then backs up, maneuvering a wheelchair up the stairs. Huge Marine. Skinny kid who looks like an AIDS patient. Jock in a football jersey. The crowd backstage parts like the Red Sea.

The whole parade could not be more absurd and I can't help but grin. I take one look at Curt and I can tell he's having fun. He's pretending to be pissed as hell, but *I know* he's having fun. There's no way he needs a wheelchair, but even that makes me grin. Leave it to Dad to keep the rules straight even when he's bending them.

They reach the top and Curt ditches the chair. He stands before me, trying to pretend he hates my guts. "Your dad fucking kidnapped me," he says at last, glancing over his shoulder. I shrug.

"We're on in two minutes."

"He made me leave the hospital and dragged me here while I still have a temperature. . . ."

"You better start if you're going to warm up, you know," I say. "They've already called 'time.' "

Ollie slides up behind me with Curt's guitar.

"You're late," he says. "And there are A-and-R guys in the audience tonight. Saw 'em up front. Two old geezers trying to dress like the Sex Pistols."

He hands Curt the guitar and it's the moment in the movie when the music swells and none of the actors say anything, but everyone knows what's going to happen.

Out front the announcer's voice is whipping the crowd into a frenzy.

"Back from the dead, for one final performance, straight from the psych ward, in the custody of the military police, with one last shot at free expression before being dragged away to jail . . ."

I look at Curt.

"We're going to be huge," I tell him. "Fuck the weatherman, we're going to be *huge!*" He gives me a weird look, but I don't have time to explain. They're calling our name. There's a chant rocking The Dump and it's our name—Rage/Tectonic. I nod at Curt.

"Let's have this conversation."

This time I lead. I slide in behind the drum set and let my huge ass sprawl over the chair. I'm the poster boy for obese drummers and I *know* I look funny. I lift my arms high above my head and hold them there, flesh dangling, waiting for Curt's signal. I have two seconds to look out over the audience. A moment of time to see all the twisted, bony, warped parodies of hands reaching for me. A flash of timelessness to see my father and brother standing backstage waiting to hear what I have to say. I have two seconds to look at Curt and see the wicked grin on his face.

Then my arms are crashing down and for the first time, live and in public, the drumsticks snap against the skins.

ACKNOWLEDGMENTS

I would like to gratefully acknowledge the artists who inspired this book: Kurt Cobain, whose life and lyrics said, "come as you are," and J. D. Salinger, who asked if we knew who the fat lady was. My special thanks to Mark Partridge, whose literary advice and musical expertise have been invaluable. I'd also like to thank my editor, Kathy Dawson, for her untiring enthusiasm, and my agent, Ginger Knowlton, for making all the phone calls. Thanks to all my fabulous readers, but especially Laura Blake Peterson, Nicole Kasprzak, Joanna Durso, Rob Pellecchia, Edward Necarsulmer, and Chris Celestino. Thanks to Kendra Davis for teaching me about the drums, and to Julie Litwiller-Shank, Dave Haldeman, Laurie Longenecker, and Mary Bettens for patiently answering my medical questions. Thanks to Maria Bedard, April Celestino, Al Smiley, and Carol Daley for their continuing belief in my work. Finally, my deepest love and appreciation go to my parents, Linda and William Going.